Beauty SLEEP

E. DAVIES

Beauty Sleep / E. Davies. – 1st ed.
ISBN: 978-1-912245-40-6

Beauty Sleep

Author's Note

This is an age gap MM romance (no age play or ABDL).

It features Briar—a 21-year-old boy whose less-than-innocent fantasies always start with a window left wide open—and Prince, the jaded 40-something Daddy who slips in and transforms from a wicked fairy to a sweet prince... with a wicked streak.

There's plenty of dirty talk and sweet dreams, including scenes of orgasm control; secret identity/disguise and anonymity; and nonverbal/limit consent.

And, of course, every Twisted fairytale ends in a happily-ever-after!

I'M AWAKE, OF COURSE.

The translucent curtains in my bedroom are fluttering softly in the warm summer breeze. Every breath of air that slips through the wide-open bay window torments my naked body. I'm flat on my back, and my rock-hard dick is twitching against my stomach.

"No," I moan half-heartedly, but I already know I don't mean it. "Not again."

Discovering my deepest desires has wrecked my life.

No amount of shoving my hands under the pillow and thinking about calculus will help. Nothing does except... well, the obvious answer. And these days, even *that* doesn't always work. I've spent hours lost in my fantasies, never quite able to spill over the edge, soaking my sheets in sweat and frustrated tears.

From the laughter and noise outside my window, it's about three in the morning. Vibes is just around the corner. I've never been, but I've heard all about the dimly-lit back room and the club nights for all tastes. A stream of men pours out of its doors at closing time, buzzing with frustration and triumph.

Right about now, my roommates will be crowding into a diner booth, sharing all the gossip before they come home at dawn.

That could be me tomorrow. Three hours ago, I turned 21, and apparently there's nowhere like Vibes on a Saturday night. My friends want me to come, too—in every possible way. But I've got a secret: my desires are too twisted to be fulfilled in the throbbing beat and dim light of the dance floor.

If only they knew what I get up to in the dark.

A stronger breeze rushes into the room. For a second, I swear I catch a glimpse of the darkened street, and shadows of people walking past, and I can hardly breathe.

Excitement flushes my cheeks and races down to the tips of my fingers. Just like that… I'm touching myself. The first brush of my fingertips against my swollen, needy shaft makes me swallow a moan.

"Fuck," I breathe out.

A couple of strokes couldn't hurt. Enough to settle myself down, right?

Ha. As if. I can't fool myself… but I can't stop myself, either. The head of my cock is glistening and wet with anticipation. I'm so turned on it almost hurts.

Maybe… maybe tonight, I *could* keep going, and it won't take long, and I'll be able to get there. After a sound night of sleep, I'll wake up feeling like myself for the first time in weeks. I won't need to guzzle coffee to survive my morning classes.

Oh, hell, why not? It's after midnight, so it's technically my birthday. And I deserve a treat. I just want to shoot my load so hard that I have to change my pillowcases.

"Mmm," I groan softly, rolling my head back. "Fuck, fuck, *fuuuck...*"

The tight ring of my fingers feels so good around my sensitive hard-on. But this gentle pace isn't going to get me there. I can barely feel a gentle touch anymore. It makes it even tougher to lose myself in the fantasy of being woken by a single fingertip stroking around my nipple, say...

Why can't it be like that first night a few months ago?

I accidentally left the window open, and I woke to a chilly bedroom and the sound of partygoers. It was just a stray passing thought: *What if a stranger sees my wide-open window? What if he does something about it?*

I've never gotten so hard so fast in my life. And that was the moment my life went downhill.

Most nights since then, I've imagined that stranger, but I don't even try to picture his face. The hot part isn't who he is. It's what he is—cocky, experienced, and certain about his desires—and what he does about it.

He'll notice the curtains fluttering and step over the low front wall into our little front yard. He'll slowly pull aside the curtains and find me here, splayed out and naked on the bed. And he'll like what he sees.

I squeeze myself firmly until electric chills of pleasure shudder their way down my spine. My cock is throbbing, but the more I try to let my mind be swamped by pleasure, the further I feel from the climax I so badly need.

Come on. Please...?

I roll onto my side, my back to the window. I imagine the soft scrape as the mystery man pushes aside the little rickety deck chair that sits outside my window. He looks around to see if anyone's watching. Then, he shoves his way through the curtain.

I hear his footfall, heavy on the wooden floor. It's all I can do to control my breathing, keep it nice and deep and even so I can pretend I'm asleep as he prowls up to me…

Damn it. I'm even more turned on now, but the build-up is too slow. This isn't going to be the quick release I was hoping for. I choke back a moan of frustration, my grip tightening around the throbbing length. The harder I go, the better chance I have of getting there. But, tomorrow night, I'll need to go even harder.

Fuck.

I wish I could recapture the feeling I had when I first discovered my deepest fantasy. With such a vivid imagination, it only took me the slightest touch, a few tugs of my wrist, and I'd sleep so well afterward.

Now I'm just exhausted all the time… and more than a little lonely.

The answer is obvious. I should deny myself for a few nights. That'll help me reset everything. The end result will be easier *and* better. But ever since I discovered this fantasy… it's apparently become impossible to deny myself. The moment I wake up with hot, ferocious need burning through my veins, I forget all my promises.

Every night, I fall into the same trap, and I tell myself it'll be different… and yet, every night, I find myself here.

I don't even care about the price I'll pay tomorrow. My fingers are curled around my stiff cock. I'm desperately pumping my hand up and down, pressing my face into the pillows as I imagine lying still for my perfect imaginary stranger.

It's only ever been a fantasy, but this fantasy is all I want.

Not writhing in pleasure on the dance floor as laser beams and hands slide across my bare skin. Not dimly-lit back rooms where men wear and wield leather. Not messaging strangers on all the apps, trying to find someone to invite in. I want someone to stumble upon me and sweep me away with the force of his desire.

And someday, my stranger will come—in more ways than one. But for tonight, it's just me, the open window, and my forbidden dreams.

CHAPTER
One

BRIAR

"Heads up, birthday boy!"

A shot glass whizzes across the bar and slides to a halt right in front of me.

"Oh," I stutter, my cheeks burning. I have no idea what alcohol's in there, but it's bright pink—and definitely a bad idea.

But then, I'm the motherfucking queen of the Realm of Bad Ideas.

"How'd you know?" I look up at the tall, blond, shirtless bartender.

He just winks. "Let's call it magic. Happy twenty-first, sweetheart."

There's a little smattering of applause at that, and even a few catcalls. I blush and clear my throat, glancing around while trying to avoid catching the gaze of anyone in particular.

It suddenly feels like I'm the special of the night... and I don't know how I feel about that.

"Hey, Em!" calls out a gray-haired guy sitting at the other

end of the bar, waving down the bartender. He and his friends are all dressed up in leather, obviously going to the party at Vibes after this. "How much will you charge me to tell everyone I'm turning twenty-one, too?"

The bartender props a hand on his hip and turns to him. "My integrity is worth a small fortune, darling."

"But Em's OnlyFans is reasonably priced," one of his friends heckles. Even Em joins in the laughter, and the feeling of being watched dissipates as conversations resume around me.

Phew, I breathe a sigh of relief. *I'm glad the attention isn't on me anymore.*

That gives me a chance to raise my birthday shot to my lips for a cautious taste. To my relief, it slides sweetly past my lips, and it tastes like bubblegum.

Not bad, actually.

I sip slowly to make it last while I stare openly around, checking the place out. My friends and roommates are supposed to be showing up any time now, but obviously they aren't here yet. They're allergic to arriving on time.

That just means I get a chance to soak up all the magic I've only ever seen from through the windows. The promise of a long, thrilling night, the smell of cologne and beer and possibility...

It's *almost* enough to make me reconsider my decision.

My friends don't know that I'm not coming to Vibes. But I swear, I really am happy just to have birthday drinks, and then make up an excuse to head home. There's no class tomorrow. I can take the whole night to indulge in my favorite fantasies... and maybe even get to the finish line this time.

Right now, I could sure use a mind-blowing orgasm or ten.

"Well, well, well," says an unfamiliar voice. The warm purr drips into my ear, making heat rise to my cheeks. "Someone's going to be the belle of the ball tonight."

"Yeah. Just call me Beauty," I snort, turning to see who it is.

Oh, shit.

This guy is older than me—probably by a good fifteen years—but he's *hot*. He's holding himself just a little further away than he has to, casually leaning one elbow against the counter. Like he could walk off at any moment.

And I'm surprised at how much I don't want him to.

The stubble across his jaw is dotted with silver hairs. His bleach-blond hair is close-cropped, and he's wearing a simple black leather jacket. His eyes are this intense, smoky gray, but there's something light and mischievous about them. His full lips are framed by laugh lines, and his jaw is sharp and stubborn.

He's the definition of a Daddy... and he's winking right at me.

"I sure will, Beauty. Which is it?"

"Which... is what?" A nervous giggle escapes me as I fidget with the empty shot glass, blushing furiously.

"A sleeping beauty, seeking the right prince to kiss him and wake him at last?" he purrs, leaning his whole weight on the bar. His forearm is on the countertop, leaving his hand just an inch or two away from mine. "Or the kind of beauty who invites a beast into his bed?"

He raises an eyebrow, but I'm still just staring at him, my jaw hanging open.

I can't believe he stumbled on my greatest fantasy within thirty seconds.

Where did he come from, anyway? I should have noticed a face like his—especially those eyes. Stormy dark gray, fine lines around them that hint at a big heart and soul... yet carefully guarded, giving nothing away.

And now I'm way too turned on to think straight.

Heat crawls up the back of my neck. My pants suddenly feel a whole lot tighter. The tingle on my skin is like a building electric charge. Sparks are gathering at my fingertips, ready to leap from my bare skin to his... the moment he touches me.

Fuck. I *want* him to touch me.

"Um..." My voice squeaks and I clear my throat, my tongue darting nervously across my lips.

"Uh huh?" This mysterious Daddy tilts his head, his eyes sparkling. He's got this beautiful, wise, quiet confidence— the kind that doesn't need to name itself out loud in order to be felt. I can feel it filling the whole damn bar right now as he watches me like he knows every thought crossing my mind.

And every desire tucked away in the back of my thoughts, where nobody can see them.

"I don't know *what* I want," I murmur, frustration rising in my chest. The words spill out before I can stop them. "And the only things I know I want... I don't think I'm supposed to. Out of the two of them, I guess that makes me Sleeping Beauty. Just waiting around for someone else to want me first. Dumb, right?"

I duck my head with mortification, bracing myself.

But he isn't laughing at me. "Beauty," he says softly instead, and I look up at him. He's smiling so gently at me that I can't help but slowly relax. "It's not an either-or. You get to try both… and the right man can *be* both."

Holy shit. I've never met anyone who can calm me down and turn me on at the exact same moment.

The silence between us stretches out, and he's still holding my gaze. I'm squirming on the bar stool, but he won't let me look away. I can barely remember how to breathe. The only thing I can focus on anymore—besides the depths of his eyes—are his pale pink lips.

It takes all my bravery to murmur, "You're right. Thanks, Daddy."

Maybe that'll make him kiss me.

The stranger's eyes flash with amusement, and then he winks at me. "Anytime, Beauty." But instead of leaning down and kissing me, he just raps the counter softly with his knuckles. "Now, go ahead."

I squint with confusion. "Go ahead and…?" *Kiss him? Is he actually reading my mind?*

His eyes glimmer with amusement. "Try another sip," he tells me, pointing at the shot glass I'm still clutching between my thumb and forefinger. "That's the only way to figure out if you like it."

"*Oh*," I breathe out suddenly, and another nervous giggle slips free. "Oh, yeah."

Shit. I only meant to sip it. But I'm so eager to obey him that I threw the whole glass back until the shot pours across my tongue, sticky-sweet.

It burns my throat and I stifle my cough with a fist, trying desperately to play it cool despite the tears gathering in the corners of my eyes. I set the empty glass back on the counter and muffle another cough, then gulp a few times.

"Well?" He raises an eyebrow.

"Um..." I weakly cough again. "I don't know. It's okay?" He sighs at me like he's disappointed, and I frown at him. "What?"

"How *very* twenty-one," he sighs, raising his eyes to the ceiling.

"What's that supposed to mean?" I don't even have to feign indignation.

He glances over and pauses for a moment, like he's about to say something else entirely. Then he changes his mind, and all of a sudden he wryly smiles at me. "Your tastebuds haven't developed yet. Give it a decade, you won't be able to drink that stuff."

I fold my arms and stare up my nose at him. "Apparently some men *are* both. They talk like a prince, and they've got the manners of a beast."

The Daddy stares at me—and then he laughs, loud and genuine, while I grin like the cat who got the cream. "Touché. I'm just a grumpy old fairy who's tried it all before. You're only young once, Beauty. Figure out what you want by kissing them all—the princes *and* the beasts."

My friends still aren't here—there's no sign of them when I turn and glance over my shoulder—and somehow, it gives me a little more confidence. Maybe... just maybe, I can transform myself from shy, nervous Briar into a brave Beauty.

What would Beauty do? I already know the answer to that, so I clear my throat.

"I've never told anyone this... but there *is* one thing I know I want."

This could go well—or very, very badly.

CHAPTER
Two

BRIAR

I DON'T KNOW HOW I WENT FROM TONGUE-TIED TO SPILLING my deepest secrets to this Daddy.

Maybe because there's an energy about him that draws me in. He's light and layered, complex. If he were a drink, he'd be... aged whisky, I guess. And he's not wrong: I'm a basic pineapple daiquiri bitch.

Not even that—I'm a *virgin* daiquiri. I've always dreamed of making it to the cocktail page, if you get what I mean. But I've never been this excited about flirting with anyone before.

The man doesn't hesitate to set down his glass, turning to give me his full attention. "Tell me what's on your mind."

My heart's about to pound out of my damn chest. "I—I don't... um..." I murmur, blushing furiously.

"Listen," he says when I hesitate, leaning close. "Whatever you're into, I can guarantee I've seen weirder and wilder stuff at Vibes."

I crack a nervous little smile. "Yeah?" The private parties, crazy club nights, darkrooms... that's all normal in my friendship group. But my thing is different. They go out there to find fun before they come home in the dawn to sleep.

I want to go home and sleep until fun finds *me*—and uses me for his every whim, and leaves before dawn can show me his face.

Damn it. Don't get hard again. That's the last thing I need.

"M-My friends are going there tonight. They think I'm coming with them... and, um, I-I don't know if I want to." My palms are getting sweaty, so I shove them into my pockets. "Because I want to go home alone and... um..." I trail off.

I can barely look away from the eyes piercing me, studying me like a book. And of course it's turning me on even more, because I *like* to be studied. Perused at leisure, while stretched out naked on my bed in the dark...

Alone isn't the end of the story for me. It's the beginning of all my secret fantasies.

"Hey, look!" a familiar voice hollers from the doorway. "The party's started without us!"

Shit. They're here.

"What—" But before the Daddy can say another word, two of my roommates practically bowl into me, hugging me and slapping my back and waving the bartender down for drinks.

"Happy birthday!"

"You didn't think we'd forgotten, did you? We just had to get pretty."

"Hey, look—we brought along a harness for you. You'll look great in this!"

The stranger's voice easily cuts through all of theirs. "So... you were saying about going to Vibes?" He raises his eyebrows at me, and I blush furiously.

Shit.

I *did* just tell him that I don't know if I want to. And he's giving me an expectant look like he's waiting for me to tell the truth.

But Robby's already stepping in.

He's the dad friend in the group, the first one to swoop in when someone's being perved on. It's usually me, and often I don't even realize what's happening until later.

"We might be," Robby says, his voice suddenly Arctic-cold as he folds his arms like a bouncer. "But *you're* not invited."

A slow frown appears on the older man's face, and he looks past Robby to me, like he's expecting me to say something.

Shit.

"I—"

Robby breaks off my quiet protest by stepping between us, putting an arm around my shoulder. "Don't worry, babe. We've got you," Robby tells me firmly.

I blink, and then I'm being frog-marched to the other side of the bar to join the rest of our friends. While we walk, he kisses my temple. "You're fresh meat, babe. You gotta be careful tonight." Then he shoves me through a gap in the crowd.

"I—but—wait—"

"Here's the birthday boy!" Robby announces to the rest of the group.

A couple of my friends shove a champagne glass into my hand and pour it full. Someone else stealth-attacks from behind to put a stupid little foil paper birthday hat on me.

My mind is still whirling, and everyone's talking at once. They're showing off their outfits, and the different outfits they want to put me in. Apparently tonight is some kind of masquerade theme. They're all dressed up in leather, rubber, feathers, you name it.

And they all think I'm coming along, too.

Shit. I have to make up my mind now, don't I?

I swallow hard and turn to sneak a look at the other end of the bar… and a jolt of surprise shudders through me.

The Daddy is still there. And he's watching me.

As he catches my eyes, he raises his glass slightly and smiles. But it's not the warm, gentle smile that calmed me down before. This time, it's bitter, sharp-edged, even ironic… like he's laughing *at* me, not with me.

Or is that just my guilty conscience talking?

I feel shitty that my friends were rude to him. Robby definitely treated him like some kind of gross old perv for flirting with me. And the worst part is that I actually knew what I wanted, for once.

But I didn't say a word about it.

"Hey, sleepyhead." Robby snaps his fingers. When I finally look at him, he grins. "Wake up. Time for your birthday blessings!"

I'm still annoyed at everyone—myself more than anyone else—but there's no missing the wrestling match happening right now over a plastic fairy wand. I think it's part of Kurt's costume, but right now, it seems to be the hot commodity.

Theo wins the skirmish and brandishes it at me. "My turn first! May you have a year of finally, *finally* getting laid. All. The. Time. Morning and night, if it'll make you less grumpy before coffee."

I groan and roll my eyes as my friends all laugh.

"Damn it, I was going to say that," Jeff smacks his arm and grabs the wand. "A year of… uh… good grades. Straight As!"

"That *will* be real magic," mumbles Robby. I elbow him in

the ribs and he laughs, grabbing the wand for his turn. "A year of always having perfect hair."

I'm laughing despite myself, trying hard not to notice everyone else staring at us making a racket. But I kind of like that my friends don't care.

Damn it. They're assholes, but they do love me. Maybe I should just go along with them to Vibes tonight...

"Oh, that's a good one," Kurt admits. "I want that."

My skin prickles. The hair stands up on my forearms, and a split-second later, I hear a familiar voice in my ear, feel warm breath tingling against my neck.

"Sleep-walking is no way to live, Beauty."

Damn it. He's right. I duck my head and blush furiously. I want to apologize, but I can't even look him in the eye.

"Hey!" Robby whirls around and glares at him, puffing out his chest as he strides up to me again. "I told you before. You're not invited to the party, pal. I can write it on a Post-It note if you need help remembering, old man."

I wince, silently pleading with Robby not to be catty, but he's not looking at me.

"He doesn't want to talk to you, okay?"

I mean, it's sort of true. I want him to take liberties without even talking to me. But he doesn't know that.

The Daddy isn't even looking at Robby. His piercing gray eyes are fixed on me again. I feel like a bug pinned to a card. I'm pretty sure he can hear every one of my thoughts—and it makes me squirm on the spot.

My friends are waiting for this man to talk. And he's waiting for me to say it's okay—to admit to them that I like whatever strange spell he's casting on me. Or even to admit to them that I know what I want, and it's not what they think I want. Or that I'm not as innocent as they all think.

But I can't, and I don't.

"My turn for birthday blessings," the Daddy says at last, disappointment written all over his features. "May you wake up *before* you go out on the scene. Otherwise, you'll wake up one day and find that they've plucked every... last... petal."

Then, he zips up his leather jacket and walks away.

Shit.

I want to apologize, to run after him. But I'm frozen to the spot. A shiver runs down my spine, and I stare at the back of his retreating head. He just walks straight through the crowd and out the door, disappearing into the night.

I can hardly breathe.

That sounded like... like some kind of curse.

"Well," Robby finally says, a little too brightly and loudly. "That was weird. You all right?"

I shake my head and raise my shoulders in a little *what the hell?* shrug, accepting the drink he presses into my hand. "Yeah...?" I murmur, even though I'm not sure.

Conversations are starting and drinks are disappearing, but there's one thing I'm finally sure about: I don't want to go to that party. And if I've learned one thing from tonight... it's that I should say so, before it's too late.

"You know, I'm going to go home, actually." I'm braced for the groans and wheedling, and this time I don't let myself give in. "I didn't really sleep last night." At least that's the truth.

"You *never* sleep," groans Robby. "Are you sure, man? You don't have to miss out on your twenty-first birthday. We can get you a Red Bull."

"Believe me, I can't *wait* to get in bed," I promise them, laughing.

"It takes all kinds of people," says Theo. "Even the weirdos."

"And you guys should know," I counter, kissing Robby on the cheek and hugging Theo. That starts the round of goodbye hugs, overruling their protests. "Enjoy the night for me, huh? Tell me all about it tomorrow!"

At last, I'm stepping out of the bar and into the cool night. I'm heading home alone, like I'd planned to. I just didn't expect to feel this disappointed about it.

I guess this is what it feels like to get what you want... and then realize you didn't really want it after all.

And it's nobody's fault but my own.

CHAPTER
Three
PRINCE

People forget that the ugly duckling has feelings, too.

I've long since learned how to make up for my shortcomings. I can talk to anyone and get them to smile, even laugh. But the vibe changes when guys realize I'm interested in them—or, worse, their friends. Then it's all cold shoulders and "you can do better" whispers. And life hasn't yet taught the hot young guys how to say no kindly.

Tonight, rejection tastes more bitter than usual. I couldn't quite shrug it off as I headed home to shower, shave, and change into my outfit. I just kept finding myself thinking about Beauty. And I don't even know his real name—he never offered, and I never asked.

Maybe that's just as well, considering how it ended.

I should just embrace the role I always get cast in. I work my jaw around as I stride down the street. *They see me as a wicked old fairy? I can act like it. I could tell the door guy not to let them in...*

I sigh and shake my head, pushing my hands into my

pockets. I already know I won't do that. Beauty's friends had bad manners but good intentions. He's obviously easy to push around. There's a reason he called me Daddy right away—he's so obviously the kind of boy who needs someone to call the shots.

If he doesn't have a Daddy of his own, his friends are right to watch out for him. I meant what I said—he really *will* get torn apart if he goes out on the scene. And I don't get any satisfaction from knowing that. It just aches.

And I can't help wondering… before his friends arrived, what the hell was Beauty about to tell me?

"Hey, is that Prince? You on deck tonight?"

I glance around, and some guy wearing a leather hood catches my eye and waves from the other side of the street. He's a regular at Vibes. He must recognize me, even behind my feathered mask, from the rest of my outfit: black velvet trousers and silk floral-patterned waistcoat.

Add a great sense of style to the list of things I've got going for me.

My DJ persona kicks in automatically. "Your Prince is coming for you, darling," I answer, my voice just aloof enough, yet honeyed and suggestive. "As long as you come for me. Bottom floor, from twelve to two."

The guy laughs, gives me a thumbs-up, and turns back to his friends. And despite myself, I can't help smiling. More people know me by my DJ name than my legal one these days—and I like it that way.

I never tell people where it came from.

When I was Beauty's age, I looked in the mirror and I hated what I saw. I used to hold myself back from even trying, because what was the point? My only hope was that

I'd get hotter with age, like some fairy godmother would come along, wave her wand, and transform me into Prince Charming.

Then the years passed and I realized that if I have a fairy godmother, she has a Hitachi for a wand, and she lost the charger in another dimension.

Honestly, who can blame her? We've all been there. And I've found my own ways to stand out. In a dark room with the beat pumping, it doesn't really matter what I look like—only how I perform.

So to speak.

Ugh. After my set, it's my best chance to get laid, but I can't even get excited about it tonight. That gorgeous, shy, maddeningly timid boy really has gotten into my head. And I won't even see him at Vibes… unless he was too timid to tell his friends what he really wanted.

Again.

I work my jaw around, trying to push away the feeling of disappointment as I shove my hands into my pockets.

It isn't even that Beauty didn't stand up for me. Or that I'm older than him—that's just a fact. I happen to know my extra years have blessed me with a deficit of fucks to give about what the infants call me.

I'm just upset because I've spent half my life being ashamed of wanting beautiful men when it's so obvious that I'm not in their league. So I know exactly what it looks like when someone is too ashamed of their desire to stand up for what they want.

That Beauty boy has to smarten up.

That's all I told him when we parted ways—in my own way. If that makes me wicked, so be it. Every Daddy knows that being mean is sometimes the kinder option. It's far better than letting Beauty sleepwalk down an even worse path than mine.

Men didn't hesitate to tell me no. But Beauty is pretty enough that they'll say yes on his behalf, and if he's not careful, he'll never learn how to want anything for himself. He'll just get chewed up and spat out by the scene in a few decades, with no more of an idea who he is.

Ugh. Now my heart hurts when I'm supposed to be having a good night.

I lift my head, looking around for a distraction. It's probably futile. I know this street—all the houses have tiny, cobblestone front yards. A few flower pots are about as interesting as it gets around here. There's one house with a rickety folding chair outside the window, but I've never seen anyone sitting there…

Wait.

Holy shit. Of all people, it can't be… but it is.

It's Beauty.

He's got his head tipped back to look at the sky. He hasn't noticed me yet, but I can recognize his features even in the dim evening light. And that inexplicable magnetic attraction is already pulling me straight toward him.

What do I have to lose?

Beauty is sprawled on the little black metal folding chair. He's leaning back on two legs, resting the back of his head against the window frame to gaze at the night sky. His feet are resting on the low wall right next to me. In those little black faux leather shorts, his legs look miles long—and it's a journey I'm dying to take.

Fuck. My heart is hammering against my ribcage.

My black velvet pants suddenly feel that much tighter. I can barely suppress my urge to run my palms along the outsides of Beauty's calves, over his knees, on and on up to his thighs…

God. Are these pockets deep enough to subtly adjust myself?

But it's not just my body responding to him. It's a lot weirder than that.

These tingles are shivering along my spine. The hair on the back of my neck practically stands up, like it's trying to alert me to something important. My heartbeat is still pounding in my ears, and the world is narrowing until all I can see is Beauty.

I just want to study every single thing he says and does. Like there's something in me that he needs… and vice versa, that's the weird part.

What does this boy have that I need so badly? I don't know, but I'm dying to find out.

The first words spill out of my mouth before I can even think twice about them. "That's not very safe, you know."

Beauty turns his head to look at me. I brace myself for whatever he'll say when he recognizes me… but he's just staring at me with a little wrinkle between his brows.

Holy shit. He doesn't know who I am with my mask on.

In a split-second, I've already made my decision: I'm not going to tell him. Not yet, anyway. Second chances don't come around every day.

"Sitting like this?" Beauty finally says, easing his feet off the top of the wall. His chair tips forward again to rest on all four legs. "Thanks, Daddy," he bats his lashes at me and pouts. "Your wisdom has saved me from a surefire concussion."

Sassy little thing. God, I like it. All the things I want to do to that pretty, faux-innocent face just slam into my brain at the same time.

"I was going to say leaving those legs lying around like that." I rest my hand on top of the wall. "But the concussion risk is worth noting."

Beauty's cheeks turn pink as he giggles. "Dressed like that, I bet you're going to the ball. You'll see plenty of legs there. You don't need mine."

"Maybe I just want them, then." I'm using my work voice now—the low, sultry purr. Might as well fully play the part behind my mask. "So, what's a beauty like you doing *not* going to the ball?"

Beauty looks surprised for a moment, and I pause to see if he recognizes the nickname. But he doesn't—he just blushes.

Maybe I'm laying it on a little thick, but I've already left enough marks on the poor boy for one night with my sharp tongue. Now, I just want him to giggle and blush and feel as good as he's supposed to on his own birthday.

"I don't know," he murmurs. "The scene isn't my thing."

Behind my mask, I raise my eyebrows as I check my watch. I only have about five minutes before I really *have* to leave.I hope he doesn't think he's all sweet and vanilla, because that's not enough time to break the news to him: he's obviously not. My gut tells me that much.

I just don't know what he's into yet.

"What is, then?"

I step right over the low wall and sink down to sit on it, and Beauty gasps. Then he starts squirming with excitement, wrapping his feet nervously around the legs of the chair— and, in the process, spreading his legs.

God. The things I want to do to him, right here and now…

"Um…" Beauty stutters.

I grin and lean toward him, bracing my elbows on my knees. "If you're too embarrassed to say it, you can whisper it into Daddy's ear."

He makes this adorable little squeaking noise, and then he shakes his head slightly. He just turns in his chair and looks at the open window behind himself, and then at me, and then back to the window, and then the ground again.

"I—I like—I mean…"

Come on, I urge him mentally, trying to swallow my impatience. *Tell me what you want. You can do it just this once. It'll get easier next time.*

He bites his lip. He's looking up at me slowly, so shyly that I want to wrap him in my arms and hold him until his nervous jitters fade away. But I hold myself back and wait a little longer… and then he clears his throat.

"You know Sleeping Beauty?" he murmurs. "I, um… I leave the window open. So a prince can come."

Then he ducks his head and stares at his lap, twisting his hands together firmly.

I lean back, resting my hand on the wall next to me. As I think, I walk two fingers along the wall beside me, down my thigh to my knee.

He likes to go to bed early. He likes anonymity, but not big parties. And he's waiting for a prince to come…

"Oh," I breathe out, because *now* I get it, and it all seems stunningly obvious.

Beauty makes a tiny sound of embarrassment and peeks up at me. I just grin slowly at him, leaning forward to let my fingertips hop over to his knee. It's warm and electric under my fingertips… and I want *so* much more.

"Yeah?" Beauty breathes out softly. His whole body shivers at the touch. His thighs spread even further apart as he goes perfectly still. He even closes his eyes most of the way, turns his cheek away… like he wants to pretend he's sleeping.

That's what he wanted to tell me at the bar. Oh, yeah. It all makes sense now.

"So, what does this Beauty dream about while he sleeps?" I murmur. His eyes fly wide open as he stares at me. I slowly but mercilessly let my fingertips walk up his thigh, not even giving him a chance to answer. "A prince who steals what he wants in the moonlight?"

The hard line in Beauty's shorts tells me that I'm on the right track—and so does his face. He doesn't say a word, but he's glowing with hope and delight and nervous excitement.

"To sleep, perchance to dream…" I grin wickedly.

Beauty looks almost ready to leap to his feet and flee inside. He makes a tiny little sound. Then he reaches down to pinch his own thigh, like he's checking if he's dreaming.

It's as sweet as it is hot.

"Mmhmm?" I grin, sliding my fingers up to pinch him in almost the exact same spot.

"Ow! I already did that," he pouts at me.

Whew. This boy really hasn't had anyone take charge properly before. He's got a lot to learn.

"So?" I ask with a laugh, and Beauty's cheeks go red.

He stutters wordlessly. The way he folds his hands between his thighs and gazes down is the very picture of excited submission. It's adorable how excited he is. He can't contain himself—even his toes are wriggling in his flip-flops.

Looks like tonight is going to turn out well after all.

"The night is young, and I have a lot to do," I tell Beauty. "I think you should head inside before you catch a chill. Get some sleep, while you can."

As I stand up, he leaps to his feet. "Are… are you coming back…?" he asks, still adorably shy.

"Are you going to leave the window open tonight?"

Beauty's eyes shine with excitement as he nods so hard that his chair rattles, and my chest swells up like a damn balloon. Despite all my cynicism, I can't help smiling. After the way our last encounter ended, this reaction is exactly the flattery I needed. Then, like he hardly dares to ask but he can't help himself, Beauty murmurs, "How quiet will you be?"

"You'll find out," I tell him with another wicked smile. "Or perhaps you won't, if I'm quiet enough."

Beauty makes this strangled moaning noise that turns into a breathless, nervous giggle. "Well, now I don't know how I'll get to sleep."

"Chamomile tea," I deadpan, stepping back over the wall. "Or find a contract to read." I lift my chin slightly in farewell. "Good night, Beauty. Sleep tight."

"I will," he breathes out, and then he dives straight through the window and tugs the curtain closed.

Poor Beauty. I don't think there's enough chamomile on Earth.

I stay where I am for a few moments and count down the seconds in my head.

Ten, nine, eight—

On five, the curtain wobbles. On three, I catch him peeking at me, and I give him a slow smirk.

He makes another of those strangled little noises as he

lets the curtain fall again, and then scurries away from the window. My ribs hurt from holding back my laughter as I finally turn away.

It's not just the mask that helps me hold my head high as I walk down the street and into Vibes. It's the glowing knowledge that there's a boy out there waiting for a Daddy—waiting for me.

And I know exactly what to do.

I can't believe my luck.

A prince has finally come, and he's left me with dirty promises, weak knees, and an insatiable hard-on.

Forty-four, forty-five... wait. Was I on the forties or the fifties?

Oh, fuck it. I can't stop myself from peeking again.

I half-expect him to still be there, lingering outside all evening. Guarding his catch and tormenting me while I try to fall asleep. God, that's a hot idea. Maybe I could be into it.

With one trembling hand, I reach out to lift the curtain.

He's gone.

"Ohhhmygod," I groan, letting out a breath as I tumble onto the bed and grab my pillow, squeezing it for dear life. "Happy *fucking* birthday to me."

See? I'm not sleepwalking through life. I was just waiting for the right man to come along. If only that Daddy I met earlier could see me now.

Prince Charming is kind of like him: confident, older, and happy to call me Beauty. But this time, I made sure he knows what I want. Judging by the fact that he can get me rock-hard with just his fingertips, he's going to reward me for it later.

Fuuuck.

I have no idea what this guy looks like. Dark eyes, I think, and a sharp jawline. It's perfect. In all my hottest daydreams, I feel my prince's force, taste his sweat, and hear his growled demands… but I never get to see his face.

And the chemistry between us! I never even imagined I could feel anything like it. Every time I invited him closer, he took that liberty… and a little more, exactly the way I've always wanted. His voice drips into my ear in sultry, honey-golden tones, and I just want to close my eyes and obey every word…

"Mmmph," I moan, squirming onto my back and hastily stripping my clothes off to sprawl naked on the bed. My cock is midair, throbbing hard. Pleasurable little shivers run down my spine every time it brushes against my stomach.

"Fuck," I sigh raggedly. "Not yet. But later."

And then I let go, tugging the sheet over me as I roll onto my front again, shoving both hands firmly under my pillow. It feels good, nestling up against the mattress, but I'm not going to hump or grind.

I'm going to wait, because I have something better to look forward to.

"How the hell *am* I gonna sleep, though?"

Fuck it, I'll just lie still and pretend if I have to. The important part is that I've left my window wide open. Everything I've ever wanted is on its way, and there's nothing I can do but wait.

I really hope my prince will finally come… and that I will, too.

CHAPTER
Five

PRINCE

I can't believe I'm actually doing this.

A night on the decks always leaves me exhausted, but brimming with the desire to deliver on the promises I've been weaving around my audience like a sensual spell. And tonight, I know exactly where to go next.

I didn't hang around after my set. I barely even stopped to say goodbye to anyone before I headed straight here.

I'm leaning against the gatepost, pretending to fidget with my phone as I watch the curtains flutter across Beauty's window.

It's wide open… just like he promised.

That's a relief. I knew I was taking a risk by telling such a skittish boy that I'd come back later. I've spent the last few hours hoping that Beauty wouldn't chicken out at the last minute.

Once the coast is clear, I pocket my phone and step over the little wall into the front yard. The chair has been carefully moved aside, like he wants to make sure I won't trip over it.

My excitement is almost impossible to contain. Whether he knows it or not, Beauty has offered me the most precious gift: his deepest desires.

I want to treasure them—and him.

Slowly, I bend down and duck through the open window, stepping softly onto the hardwood floor. My eyes have adjusted to the gloom of the lamp-lit street, but the room's even darker. But I can sure as hell hear Beauty's breathing. It's so loud and ragged with excitement.

I knew he'd be awake.

The poor boy must have spent hours lying awake, tossing and turning, desperate for my touch and lost in his deepest fantasies.

I blink several times as shapes slowly begin to form in my vision. I can just about make out the edge of a dresser or a chest of drawers. From the sound of breathing, I think the bed is straight ahead of me… but I'm not in a rush.

With every passing moment, it's harder for Beauty not to squirm with excitement. And I'm happy to torment him for a little while longer. Once I take those final few steps, it'll make it even better for us both.

I wish I was that young and vulnerable again… so willing to show my desire to the world, never even thinking it could get me hurt. But when the world laughed at me, I shut down and shut them out. Until my first DJ gig last year, I watched from a distance as everyone else revelled in the magic I wanted to make.

I threw myself into my work as a security guard instead. But that job suited me, because I've always been a Daddy—a protector at heart. And I don't want to bubblewrap this boy and try to stop him from playing with the deepest sparks of fire in his soul.

This boy wants the beast to sneak in through his window, but I know what he really needs: the prince. And tonight, I'm going to give him both.

There—I can see the bed clearly, and Beauty's silhouette sprawled across it. He's lying perfectly still, face down and ass up, arms under the pillow. And he's totally naked.

This is the hottest thing I've ever done.

I cross the hardwood floor to sit on the edge of the bed, grinning as Beauty tries not to squeak with excitement. He's so bad at pretending. It's so fucking cute... but this isn't the moment to get all warm and soft.

It's time to bring this boy's filthiest fantasies to life... and some long-forgotten dreams of my own.

CHAPTER
Six

BRIAR

He's here!

I *knew* Prince Charming would come for me. I have no idea what time it is or how long I've spent lying here—face-down, ass-up, arms folded under my pillow—listening and waiting.

And I've been on my best behavior: I only fingered myself enough to get lubed up and ready for him. Despite how achingly hard I am, I haven't been touching myself. Not even a sneaky grind against the bed.

I can barely think straight. Every soft footfall makes the floorboards creak, and my hard-on throb with excitement.

With my face in the pillow and the darkness of the room, there's no way I can see my mysterious prince. But adrenaline is flooding my body, leaving my other senses keener than ever.

The footsteps stop next to me, and the bed sinks gently.

Ohmygodohmygodohmygod.

This is hotter than all of my fantasies put together—and it's actually happening.

Even with my nose buried in the pillow, I can smell just a hint of citrus cologne and leather. Goosebumps run along my forearms, right up to the back of my neck. And my hair isn't the only thing standing on end.

As my semi swells into a full-on erection, it takes everything I've got to stay still. I swear I can feel the heat radiating from Prince Charming. I'm glowing from head to toe with hot, nervous anticipation...

And holy fuck, does it feel good. I can't believe I never even thought to fantasize about this part. I always thought the best part would be waking up to find myself lost in helpless pleasure, ravaged by a mysterious stranger.

But Prince Charming is taking his time. It's so drawn out—so tortuously, deliciously slow. I might just go crazy before he even lays one finger on me. Every passing second melts more of my brain into a hazy, eager puddle of goo.

The tense charge in the air is like lightning dancing through my bones. Every detail is burning itself into my brain. My throbbing dick, racing thoughts, the struggle to keep my breathing slow as my heart pounds at a mile a minute...

Where is he going to touch me? And how? And when?

I have no idea, and I'm so fucking excited about that, because I'm getting what I've always wanted: the chance to give up control. He'll do everything, and I can do absolutely nothing—just lie still and take it.

My cock twitches against the flat plane of my stomach, and I gulp quietly.

Oh!

Prince Charming is gently touching the back of my neck with his fingertip. Then he trails his touch straight down my spine, full of possessive intent, yet slow and soft like he really is trying not to disturb me.

Hoooly fuck. My head is spinning, and every muscle is taut and quivering with pleasure. The quiet, forceful certainty of my real Prince Charming beats all my fantasies of getting hauled around and groped.

His finger reaches the curve of my ass. I can't stop myself from a tiny little squirm of delight. Then I press my lips together hard, scolding myself.

Stay still, Briar. Jesus. You literally have one job.

I try my best to turn it into a little unconscious movement, like I'm just stirring idly, but Prince snorts with obvious amusement.

Fuck.

He already knows I'm awake. He's just making me keep playing along to embarrass myself for his entertainment. And I don't know why, but that makes it even hotter. I'm so desperate for him to tease me while I can't do a thing.

We both know I love being this kind of helpless.

I made sure my face would be hidden in my pillow so I couldn't see anything. All my other senses seem that much sharper as a result. The sound of clothes rustling, for example, is easy to pick out against the street noise outside.

And the *zzzzip* as Prince Charming unzips his pants, sending my imagination wild.

Is he still fully dressed, his stiff boner poking through the folds of fabric?

Does he have one fist closed around his hard-on, already ready and waiting to push into me?

Or is he still growing thick and hard in his palm, jerking himself off to the sight of my naked body as he prepares to use me the way I so desperately hoped for?

Yes yes fuck yes c'mon please touch me more, please please fuck me, oh my god do something please I'm going to go crazy if you keep this up...!

"Lube," Prince Charming breathes out softly.

"B—"

Wait, shit, fuck.

I press my lips together hard, hoping the pillow muffled the tiny escaped sound. But there's a deep chuckle from above me as the bed shifts under his weight, and he grabs the lube from the bedside table.

He really is tormenting me, and I really do love it.

Prince kneels across my thighs. Warm velvet brushes against my bare skin, and it's enough to make the flying sparks turn into a wildfire.

Oh fuck...!

A wet fingertip trails from the small of my back, straight down over my tailbone, between my cheeks...

His warm fingertip brushes against my hole, and I'm choking back a moan.

Ohmygodohmygooood it's happening...!

This is the first time I've had anyone else inside me. I'm already lubed up and stretched out, so it barely even stings as his fingertip slides gently into me.

Prince can feel how ready I am, and he snorts with amusement. But, to my surprise, he still isn't jumping straight to the action. He just works his finger into me, tortuously slow and gentle. Almost like he really *is* trying to go undiscovered.

I've had plenty of experience with my own toys and fingers, but it's never been like this.

Just not knowing what's going to happen makes it so much hotter. Waves of arousal wash over me, burning my cheeks and tingling in the pit of my stomach. With every pump of my heart, blood surges to my already-stiff cock. The slightest touch might just make me go off like a rocket. Forget washing my pillowcases—my ceiling is in danger.

Prince's finger feels good—really good—but he's taking so long to make sure I'm ready. Is he being sweet and gentle on purpose? Or is he planning to use me mercilessly?

God, I hope it's the latter, because I've never been this hard in my life.

Oh, fuck!

The white-hot stretch of a second finger inside me feels too incredible for words. I bite the pillow hard as Prince starts fucking me with his fingers, slow and deep. The room is spinning around me, and I'm sinking deeper and deeper into his spell.

Then I feel a hand closing around my cock, stroking me gently.

What if I can't cum?

Shit.

I tense up, and just like that, I'm drowning in the all-too-familiar desperation, frustration, and a sinking feeling that I know exactly what's going to happen. Just like last night. It took forever to get to sleep after I finally gave up, miserably exhausted, both wrists sore, covered in sweat… and more desperate than ever.

Prince's fingers slid out of me. "Is something wrong?" he murmurs.

Fuck.

I want to tell him that nothing's wrong except the way I feel so *empty* all of a sudden, and I need him inside me right the fuck now.

But I also still want to keep the fantasy going, so I stubbornly bite my tongue.

Prince chuckles softly, resting a warm hand on my thigh. "I'll do as I see fit with you. But you have to tell me if there's anything you want... and if anything's wrong."

Oh. Oh, that's actually really sweet. And hot. Should I tell him? Maybe he could help. But then I have to stop pretending to be asleep...

I squeeze my eyes shut against the pillow. The more I wrestle with my frustration, the more it grows... until it finally boils over and I can't stop the words anymore. "I've been doing it too much," I moan, squirming with embarrassment as I cling to the desperate hope that he knows how to help.

"Doing what?" Prince murmurs, gently stroking my thighs.

I whimper under my breath. "Jerking off," I mumble. "I have to go so hard now. And even then, I can't always finish. I usually don't. It's like I need more and more and more..." My hands are fists against the pillow as my chest goes tight. "And I can't say no to myself. And now I've ruined this fantasy, too—"

"Shhh," Prince whispers above me. I cling to his voice and his touch like a lifeline, slowly relaxing as he strokes his hand across my thigh in slow, gentle moves, like he really is lulling me to drift off again. "All life is a fantasy, Beauty. Just stay in it for me, and I'll give you what you need, my sleeping Beauty. You don't even have to talk to me. Just lie there and take it."

Fuuuck.

I can practically hear him smiling down at me through

the darkness as he touches me so sweetly and says such filthy things…

And, just like that, we're back in the moment.

My body knows what to do. I let my breath out, sinking into the bed again as every muscle loosens at once. The excitement of the unknown is sweeping me straight off my feet and into unknown waters.

"That's it, my Beauty," he praises me in a soft murmur. "Good boy."

Something nudges against my entrance. I tense up with excitement and anticipation… but it's Prince's fingers again. He pushes them inside again, fingering me slowly and gently and ignoring whatever soft sounds slip from my throat.

I'm giving over my body and my pleasure to him until even time slips away.

The only thing that brings me back into the moment is the feeling of his fingers sliding out and the sound of foil ripping. Then, there's a blunt, thick heat against my entrance, and I bite the pillow as hard as I can.

Yes, yes—oh fuck! Yessss…!

The head of his cock pushes into the tight ring, stretching me open as my head spins. I've waited so long for this moment, and now all my deepest dreams are coming true at once.

It takes me a minute before I can take any more of his rock-hard arousal into me. It's so much bigger than his slender, meticulous fingers. But then I'm trembling, relaxing, breathing out into it.

"Relax, my Beauty. Sleep. It doesn't matter what you do. I'll still find a way to slip inside in the dead of night, and do everything you've ever dreamed of."

Holy fuck, holy *fuck, holy fuck* is that hot…!

My cock throbs steadily as I stifle my whimper, doing my best to relax around him as he pushes further and further inside.

"Just lie there and take it," Prince Charming whispers as he pushes his body into mine, splits me open, and makes it feel ten times as good as I imagined. "That's a good boy. Fuck," he groans. "So… fucking… tight…!"

Inch by inch, he sinks into me. I'm aching with the desire to buck into him, to press my back against his chest and squirm. This strange, dizzying heat is building inside me as every thrust makes the head of his cock slide across the spot inside that feels the very best.

I'm yielding to him as he fills me up, stretches me past bursting, further than I ever would have thought I could go.

It's *so* fucking *good…!*

I press my lips together to bite back my whimper as he sets into a real rhythm now. With every rock of his hips, my body falls under his spell—from my breathing to my heartbeat, I can't do anything but anticipate each surge of his hips as his hard dick fills me past bursting.

It's literally the hottest thing ever. Every inch of my skin is so fucking sensitive. The tiniest brush of his hand and I'm on fire, trying not to ripple and arch into his touch.

And Prince Charming is still taking it slow and steady, like he really is taking everything he wants while trying not to disturb me. It's almost too good, the truth of what's happening layered with the fantasy we're playing at...

This way, I don't have to want anything. He just gets to take it all, and there's not a single thing I can do about it.

And it's perfect.

I'm glowing with ecstasy. Tiny moans escape my throat, and he pretends not to hear them over the wet noises of our bodies slapping together in this slow tease of a rhythm. And I just can't believe I've gone from overstretched to needing it faster and harder.

Every time he pushes his whole length into me, his balls slap against my skin and my head whirls. Fuck, fuck, *fuck*, I can't stop myself much longer…! I'm baring my teeth, trembling under him. As I stretch out along the bed, he forces my thighs closed with his knees and keeps on pushing deep inside me.

Finally, he slams into me just hard enough that I can't stop myself. I throw my head back with the force of the delirious, ecstatic moan that seems to rip from my very throat.

"Mmmmngh…!"

And everything changes.

"Hello, there, Beauty," Prince growls, grabbing the hair at the back of my head as his pace speeds up. "I'm Prince Charming. Nice to meet you."

"Oh my fuck—oh my—fuck—fuuuuck…!" I cry out as he fucks me deep and rough. He slams into me and I cry out, trying to work my hands out from below the pillow.

But I can barely even reach behind myself before he grabs both wrists and pins them over my head. He covers my mouth with his other hand, and he just keeps on riding me hard and fast, like there isn't a second to lose.

"Nnngh!" I cry into his palm as my whole body tenses up. My eyes snap open, and I throw my weight back into him. All it does is force him deeper into me. I can't stop the stream of grunts and whimpers against his hand.

It feels so, *so* good…!

The waves of bliss are unstoppable, cresting higher and higher. I clench around his cock, and it doesn't even slow him down. His balls slap against my ass, his cock slams deep into me, and he keeps on driving into my body—using it for his own pleasure, taking everything he wants and leaving me helpless to my own pleasure.

"Oh, fuck. I'm going to—I'm actually—ohhhh, fuck…!" Every muscle in my body clenches tight, and my voice breaks into a hoarse scream, still muffled by his palm instead of the pillow. "Yes, yes… yeeees!"

My own wet, hot, sticky load spills all over the bed, my belly, everything. Every time I clamp down around him, he grunts, and my head just spins all the more. And then he lets go, wraps an arm around my chest, and grabs my hip with the other hand as he yanks out of me.

There's a moment's pause, and then…

"Yes!" Prince Charming groans through the darkness. Hot, sticky warmth spills across my lower back. I can't help whimpering with excitement even as the rolling waves of my own bliss finally begins to settle.

And, just like that, I can barely stay awake.

I mumble about laundry under my breath, and try to roll away from the wet spot. Prince grabs my hip and ignores my sound of protest, wiping me clean with a tissue before he lets me go.

Oh. That way I won't make a new wet spot. That's a good idea. "Chivalrous," I think I manage to say, but I'm not sure I got all the syllables in the right order.

Prince snorts with soft amusement. He tugs the pillow back under my head, and then with a rush of breath, he pushes himself to stand up. And before I can even moan with how much I miss the skin-to-skin contact, he puts a hand on my shoulder and squeezes with this gentle intimacy I've never felt before.

"Glad you left the window open?"

"Mmhmm." I smile sleepily into the darkness. "I'll do it again."

After a moment, Prince chuckles. "Is that an invitation?"

Yes yes yes...! All I can do is squirm excitedly against the bed until he laughs again.

"I *did* promise not to make you talk. I'll take that as a yes. But you have to let your prince give you orders, all right?"

"Mmhmm," I nod into the pillow, trying desperately to stay awake long enough to hear them.

"Good boy," Prince Charming murmurs. His hand moves to my hair, and he strokes my head once, softly, like he's untangling my curls. "Don't pleasure yourself until I return."

Holy shit.

"It may not be tomorrow night," Prince warns me. "Or even the next. Will you do that? Will you wait for me?"

I don't even have to hesitate and think about it. My prince has given me everything I wanted. So if he thinks it'll help… I'll do it.

I nod as hard as I can, only pausing long enough to stifle a yawn.

"Then leave the window open when you want me to return. Some night soon, I will." Prince rises to his feet as I smile sleepily into my pillow. "Sleep tight, Beauty. Sweet dreams."

For the first time in weeks, I don't even remember closing my eyes.

CHAPTER
Seven

BRIAR

"Good morning!" I sail past my bleary-eyed friends with a smile, grabbing a coffee mug and lifting the pot to see how much is left. "You guys actually left some for me? Happy Sunday to all!"

I turn away to grab the creamer, grinning to myself at the stunned silence. Even as I wrap my hands around the finished mug and lean against the counter, they're *still* staring.

Robby is the first to pull himself together. "Uh… in fairness, you aren't usually awake until after lunchtime."

"Arguably, not even then," Jeff adds, and they all nod in agreement.

"What can I say? I'm a new, improved Briar. Call me Briar 2.0," I wink.

"Okaaay, Briar 2.0," Robby says, raising his eyebrows and looking around at our other roommates, each of whom shrugs in turn.

"I just…" Kurt's sitting at the dining table, holding a

spoonful of Cheerios midair as the milk slowly drips back into the bowl. "What…?"

"Careful," I point. "You're about to get a little something on your shirt. Speaking of which, how was last night?"

Everyone cracks up. I set my coffee mug down on the table, fetching my textbooks from the living room. I'm so not walking right today, but nobody seems to be noticing. They're just regaling me like usual with all the stories from the club.

Nobody's ever in charge of said stories, so I let the rapid-fire excited chatter wash over me.

"—Robby found these two bears—"

"—there was this guy wearing a mask like that guy from Princess Bride—"

"—waiting for him in the dark room—"

"—a weekend retreat to become, and I quote, multi-orgasmic—"

"Huh, wow," I mumble automatically whenever the moment seems right. To be honest, I'm not really following the thread of any of their stories. I'm pretty distracted by the pleasurable ache between my legs as I slowly sit down at the table.

I've got good reason to wince a little. Thinking about that reason—and the man who wields it—makes it *so* hard not to grin like the cat who got the cream.

Or the Sleeping Beauty who got his Prince Charming.

"Hold on," Robby shushes the rest of them. "Hey, Briar."

Shit. My heart skips a beat as I glance up over my books, trying not to look too guilty. Did they notice me walking funny? Do I look less innocent than I used to be? Am I emanating the radiant, relaxed, well-rested glow of a freshly-fucked boy?

Robby frowns. "You don't feel like you're missing out on anything, do you? You know you can come whenever you want, right?"

"Huh?" I blink at him. They're definitely not supposed to know about Prince Charming's rules…

"Your birthday, man. I don't know *anyone* who didn't go out and get trashed on their twenty-first."

Theo nods earnestly. "We felt really bad ditching you to go to the club. We almost came back to check on you."

I could almost laugh in their faces with relief, but the real concern they're showing is too touching. My laugh fades into a smile.

"No," I promise them all sincerely. "I had a great night, and I got about twice as much beauty sleep as all of you combined." I scan all of my friends' faces, and then I smirk and toss my head as I add, "Obviously."

That breaks the tension with a laugh. Robby snorts and tosses a napkin at me, which I bat away.

"Dickhead," Theo grins.

I wink at him. "But a beautiful dickhead," I run my fingers through my hair and pat my cheeks, opening the top textbook in the stack. "Shiny, healthy, and radiant as the noon sun."

"Are you studying? *You?* On a Sunday, before noon?" Robby's look of concern is back.

"Yep," I chirp at him, giving away nothing.

Don't get me wrong, it's like throwing a nickel at a student loan's worth of sleep debt… but compared to usual, I feel better this morning than I have in months.

"Mr. *I'm going to flunk this test because the teacher says so, and there's nothing I can do about it,* studying," Theo shakes his had.

Robby grunts in agreement. "What the *hell* got into him? Can we get some of that?"

Not a chance.

The intensity of my wave of jealousy surprises me. But in all my years of fantasizing about the magical first time... I didn't think I'd enjoy it so much, or that it would be so sweet and tender afterward.

I don't even know what Prince Charming looks like, much less how to find him again. All I can do is wait for him to show up again.

There's nothing for me to get wrong. It's all up to him.

I can't text him a million times today and scare him off. I can't stalk his Facebook profile and decide how many kids we're having. I can't even imagine my first name with his last name. I just have to wait.

As hard as it's going to be tonight—in more ways than one—I also can't wait.

"Maybe Gay Jesus took the wheel because Briar's an inch away from failing this prereq," Robby grunts. "And he keeps sleeping through our study hours. And the big test is this week."

Actually, that's a good point. I'll never focus on my homework if I'm thinking about him all day long.

"You know, I've got an idea," I tell them, bouncing to my feet to slam my textbook closed and drain the rest of my coffee. "Group coffee-slash-study sesh at the cafe."

"*Sesh?*" Theo groans loudly, folding his arms on the table and plopping his head down on them.

"Sesh," I repeat firmly. "Now, get off your asses and get dressed. The special is half-price before ten AM. And I happen to know this weekend's special is that fruity little blueberry number you all love."

Robby groans. "Fuck. I *do* love that fruity little blueberry number. With whipped cream. But first, who are you and what the fuck have you done with the real Briar?"

"I couldn't possibly say." I grin as I gather my armful of textbooks. "You guys in or what?"

"Fiiiine," Theo sighs. "Give me ten minutes." He winces and hunches down over his folded arms again as I turn to head for my room. "Or twenty, and a blowjob."

"Ten, no blowjob, and a fruity little blueberry number. Final offer," I call over my shoulder.

I'm not so far down the hall that I can't hear Robby saying, "Guys… I've changed my mind. That boy needs *less* sleep. Anyone want to take turns waking him up tonight?"

But I'm feeling great. For the first time in months, I'm not just going along with what other people want.

I'm not sleep-walking through life. I'm awake, and I'm *slaying.* I don't know how long this will last, but until my next sleepless night, I'm going to take full advantage of it. And for once, everyone else can come along for the ride.

I feel like I've been brought back to life to discover I'm the queen of my own goddamn life.

Last night, I made my deepest, most secret dream come true. The only hard part now is going to be waiting for my Prince to return. Tonight will be the real test. Compared to that, everything else in my life is a piece of cake with a half-price, fruity little blueberry number on the side.

And extra whipped cream.

Mmm. I can't wait.

CHAPTER
Eight
PRINCE

"WAIT A MINUTE. THEY FUCKING CUT ME FROM MY *OWN* night?"

I'm used to scanning the email lists of DJs for the next month of Vibes events and not seeing my name. But this is just a shit sundae with a cherry on top.

I roll over in bed, thumbing at my screen to go back to the top of the email. Darren, Vibes' general manager, sent it at four in the morning. I floated to bed on such a high last night that I didn't bother looking at my phone until I woke up.

I wish I'd put it off a little longer. I woke up feeling *dreamy*—with the kind of morning wood that practically threatens my ceiling's structural integrity and a big smile on my face. Needless to say, that's gone now.

"Jesus." I toss my phone down on the bed, rubbing my palms over my face. "Kick me harder in the nuts, Darren."

I usually get along well with Darren. Last night, he was all panicked about cancelling Friday's private event after some organizer drama, so I suggested the theme I've been pushing him to do for months: Twisted Fantasies.

As I told him, it's all the fun of last night's masked ball, with even *more* potential for outrageous outfits and depravity. And it's absolutely perfect for my DJ brand: equal parts risqué high art and filthy piggy raunch.

Everyone's going to see the photos from tonight on Insta or Snapchat or whatever. Capitalize on the FOMO, I urged him.

Looks like Darren took my suggestion—and my whole concept—and forgot where it came from. They aren't even sticking me in the "exclusive" room—AKA, a shitty little side room that gets next to no footfall.

Wait a sec. There's another email from Darren. The subject line says *Friday*, and it was sent at four-thirty in the morning.

I scramble to pick up my phone again. This better be an apology, or at least an explanation. Maybe Darren made a mistake. Or he forgot that I told him I can sell the night out. After years working the door, my networks are bigger than anyone else suspects.

Hey Prince,

> *Can you work the door this Friday? I know this isn't what you were hoping for, but I trust you more than anyone... we all know it's the door culture that makes or breaks a night...*

> *Thanks a million,*

> *Darren*

Talk about adding insult to injury.

"Oh, fuck *off.*"

I angrily swipe out of the email before I can respond with any of the choice words that come to mind first.

Four rooms, six DJs, and almost all of them are infants who probably couldn't work out how to press play on a first-generation iPod. But they're pretty and twenty-something, which draws a crowd.

Judging by the attached graphics—probably made by Darren in Paint at 3:57am—they all like to be shirtless.

I start to dismiss my notifications one at a time, violently enough to send them flying into another state. "They'll probably paint historically inaccurate chainlink armour on their sculpted torsos," I grumble. "And it'll work."

At least there's one name I'm happy to see on the list: DJ Quarrel. The legend otherwise known as Benji Smith-Keyes is one of my best friends. We've been friends for longer than either of us can remember, and he's been DJing for about the same amount of time. He's the one who helped me break in.

And, if I'm not mistaken, a text just arrived from him… something about how it's easy to play him?

I need the tea. Anything to distract me.

"Oh, holy crap. That's a wall of text. Jesus and Dorothy and Buddha save me," I mutter. "I need coffee for this."

I have a rule against loungewear in public, so I push myself up and head to my drawers. I set my phone on top of the dresser to start reading while I rummage for a nice shirt and matching socks. Or just clean socks, at this point.

QUARREL:

WTF, man???

You've been talking about that idea for months! I'm gonna kick Darren's ass into the sun, just say the word

…Or you can pretend to be me and I'll dress up as you…

> Like a 2000s comedy

> (Dibs on Renée Zellweger playing me)

That's why he's my best friend. He can make me laugh in less than twenty seconds, even when I'm pissed off. I snort, swiping to respond to that last message.

PRINCE:

> You'll be sorry when I play myself & we end up becoming besties…

Then I scroll down the wall of text, leaning against the dresser to tug my jeans on.

QUARREL:

> Then we do a big reveal and Darren falls to his knees in apology and worships your musical genius!!!

> (In the R-rated cut, he'll worship your cock as a metaphor for your musical genius)

> Just let me know and I'll brush up on my aloof sarcasm and commanding presence and steal your clothes

> It's easy to play me, just wear Crocs and have 70 thoughts per minute and say them all

As I reach the bottom, my phone buzzes with Quarrel's answer to me.

QUARREL:

> But then I get to be besties by proxy, AND she'll inhabit my psyche so deeply that we'll understand one another without words

PRINCE:

Nobody ever believes me when I tell them you're the biggest dork I've ever met

Now I have Exhibit A

QUARREL:

Did I mention there's an agent who scouts you? And your DJ career takes off? And you meet the love of your life???

(Who is definitely not Darren despite the dick-sucking apology…)

(BUT! Maybe he awkwardly interrupts the dick-sucking apology and you all laugh sheepishly but meaningfully?)

(Except Darren, because his mouth is full)

…At least we have time to workshop this, you've been single long enough

"Fucking ouch," I grumble, flipping off my phone screen.

PRINCE:

You're supposed to be making me feel better, you prick

QUARREL:

No, I'm supposed to be distracting you. Did it work?

PRINCE:

It did until you threw shade at my love life

QUARREL:

OnlyFans isn't love, darling, it's direct community support

I should tell Quarrel what happened last night. Then he'll really eat his words. But the seconds are ticking by and I'm still just staring at the keyboard, my thumbs hovering over the letters.

Why didn't I tell him last night?

We had a few minutes to talk near the beginning of the night. And sure, I left in a rush after my set, but I didn't text him anything either. Normally we share every passing thought—and horny encounter.

But this time felt different.

I don't want Beauty to be gossip fuel.

Oh. Yeah. That's exactly what it is—because that's how the scene ends up tearing people to shreds, when people pick apart other people they don't even know.

It's not just because men like Beauty are sleepwalking through life.

It's because the rest of us are secretly jealous. Most of us wish we could be a little more like them—naive and filthy-minded, innocent and full of desire… and above all, sweet.

A lot of us wish we could be that sweet, and lose the edge of bitterness we feel like we have to use to protect ourselves from the world. And even our closest friends.

I can't stop remembering last night, just before I climbed out of Beauty's window. I turned to get one more look at him, and I saw him tucked in right where I put him, under the covers, drifting off to sleep with a smile on his lips.

And the sight of it… did something to me.

There it is again.

Something is unfurling in my chest. A part of me that feels… well… a little like Beauty, actually.

Sweet.

I kept that naive part of me under lock and key, but it never quite went away. It's fizzing away—*I'm* fizzing right now, in a way I forgot I was capable of. Tentative, nervous, excited, hungry... and just young and dumb enough to think this could work.

My phone buzzes and I swallow hard, looking down at it.

QUARREL

You know what else counts as community support in this trying morning?

PRINCE

Let me guess: bringing you coffee in bed?

QUARREL

Even better: I'll meet you there in 5. I'm paying.

Jeez... he really must feel sorry for me.

But I'm not gonna turn it down. Just like I probably can't afford to turn down Friday's shift of patting pockets, scanning IDs, and keeping the waiting customers happy.

PRINCE

I'm on the way.

As I lock the front door, I shake my head and clatter down the stairs toward the street.

Why can't I just suck it up and start taking the roles I'm given?

Quarrel will tell me to fight back. There's a reason that's his DJ name. But maybe I should just be making the magic I *can* make while staying right where I've always been: hidden in plain sight.

Lost in thought, I barely notice the walk to the coffee shop. I'm just suddenly pulling the door open, scanning the room for a familiar face—and terrible Crocs—before I head to the counter.

Quarrel isn't there. But I *do* see a face that I last saw in the moonlight, looking radiant as an angel.

It's Beauty.

With all of his personal bouncers again this time—AKA, those overprotective friends. They're huddled over a table with textbooks open, heads together.

The bell jingles behind me as I let go of the door.

Shit. Beauty shifts in his seat. He's about to look up.

What if he recognizes me from the bar? Or worse still...

If I'm going to turn and run, I have a split-second to do it. But I'm stuck where I am, rooted to the spot by the memories unfolding in my body. And the sweetness of the thing that's fizzing to life in my chest, too.

I remember Beauty's moans in the night, his breathless giggles and sly smiles, his warm lips and unashamed desire, his nakedness... oh, fuck, his nakedness. He gave me everything last night without question, body and mind.

And I discovered something I've never quite believed before. I can be not just tolerated, even wanted... but *needed*. And I've waited too long, fought too many dragons, suffered too many cutting defeats to get to that place.

I can't turn and leave now.

"Whoa." The door jangles again as Quarrel almost barrels right into me. "What's the holdup?"

I can't answer him. I'm still staring at Beauty, watching as he slowly looks up at me.

Our eyes meet.

The chatter around us from his friends and mine suddenly vanishes. Or maybe I'm just not hearing it over the ringing in my ears.

Even as his lips part with surprise, he doesn't look away, and I wait for his reaction.

Anything but disappointment, please.

Beauty's face is shifting again. Something is sparkling

there. A glimmer of something mischievous and self-assured and so much stronger than anything he showed me at the bar. More like what I saw in the night—and even bolder in the light of day.

That grumpy friend of his is standing up and scowling, and Quarrel puts a hand on my shoulder. But I barely even notice, because I'm smiling at Beauty, and I'm lost in the way he smiles back.

The first time we met, I wasn't sure… but now I am. I've found a boy worth fighting for.

CHAPTER
Nine

BEAUTY

I'M FROZEN TO THE SPOT, CAUGHT ONCE MORE IN THE MYSTERY Daddy's mesmerizing gray stare.

I feel like I've been caught in my sleep, laid out perfectly for this man to do what he wishes. I can't seem to tear my gaze away. But he's not saying a word as he watches me. It's like he's toying with me, or… or something.

I can't quite figure it out, but I feel like I'm in a game of cat-and-mouse.

Sparks are shooting straight down the back of my neck to my stomach. Every inch of my skin is tingling, straight to the tips of my fingers and toes. I'm glowing so hard I can barely even pay attention to the sudden tightness in my pants.

I feel so… so alive. And it's all thanks to this Daddy whose name I don't even know.

He gave me the wakeup call that changed everything. And then, last night, I finally made a decision of my own. I chose Prince. I invited him in, and I did it because I didn't like the feeling of not going after what I want.

Robby's chair scrapes the floor as he stands up.

Shit. Robby cares about me, but can be overprotective, and twice as thorny when he doesn't know what's happening.

"Stop." I put a hand on Robby's forearm, and he glances at me with surprise. "I—um… I *want* to talk to him."

Robby gently pries his forearm out of my grip. "So do I," he tells me with a crooked grin that makes me relax. "I wasn't getting up to punch him."

"Oh." I let go sheepishly. "I wasn't sure."

Robby considers that for a second and then gives me a *fair enough* shrug. He steps clear of his chair, shoving his hands in his hoodie pockets as he awkwardly approaches my mystery Daddy. "I was a dick last night. I'm sorry."

"Thank you," the man tells Robby. His voice is hoarser than I remember it being, but a nice, familiar kind of warm that makes me relax. "You were. But it takes a lot to apologize, especially in front of your friends, so I appreciate it."

A shiver of surprised delight runs down my spine. It's the perfectly-balanced response: gentle-sharp, embarrassing Robby without tormenting him, accepting it while letting him marinate the appropriate amount.

Spoken like a true Daddy.

Robby doesn't seem to know what to do about that. "Cool," he finally says and retreats to sit down again, rubbing the back of his neck.

The Daddy nudges his friend and nods at the counter, and he heads off to order coffee for them both.

Then he walks straight for me.

Fuck. I'm beginning to think this man really *is* a fairy. He's sure showing up at all the right moments.

Be cool, be cool, be cool...

Fuck. I didn't plan for this. I know I need to apologize...

but I haven't planned what to tell him. Or what I can say in front of my friends, who are grinning at me like a pack of Cheshire cats.

I shoot them a sideways glare. Throats clear and pages shuffle as they look down at their books again, pretending not to listen.

"Hello, Beauty," the Daddy says softly as he stands next to my chair, putting a hand on the back.

Oh my god. It's almost like he has an arm around me, but not quite. I can feel the heat of his forearm just behind my shoulder. He smells familiar, in a way that makes my hairs stand on end.

My blush crawls up the back of my neck, and the Daddy chuckles under his breath. He knows exactly how much he's teasing me.

"Enjoyed your twenty-first birthday?"

I look so far up at him that I almost crick my neck.

"Yeah." I can't help smiling back at him, biting back a grin. I really, *really* wish I could tell him just how much. "But, uh… there is one thing."

"Oh?"

I swallow hard. Better get this out of the way with. "I'm sorry, too. That I didn't stand up for you." He stares at me with surprise as I lace my fingers together nervously against my thigh, under the table. "I wanted you at my party."

His smile turns soft and gentle as he dips his head slightly. "Thank you. But no need to apologize. I know what I'm getting into, Beauty."

Shit. It's weird hearing him say that name again.

Now all I can think about is Prince moaning that name into my ear as my skin glows with a sheen of sweat, and our bodies move as one in the darkness…

"Is—Is it that easy to read me?" I stutter, my cheeks hot as hell.

His eyes crinkle with far too much amusement. "Yes," he says. "And, seeing as we're all apologizing… I'm sorry for what I said. It was a little harsh."

"Don't be," I tell him without even thinking about it. "You were right. I need to do what *I* want to do."

The older man gives me an amused shrug. "It was still harsh. But I suppose every curse is a blessing in disguise, if you know how to look at it."

"Yeah." I swallow back the lump in my throat as I smile up at him. "And every bad dream can become a good one."

Without him, I wouldn't have been brave enough to talk to Prince Charming, to invite him inside… to wake up and smell the roses.

"But you can't just dream forever. Sometimes you gotta wake up and make those dreams come true."

"Good advice," says the Daddy's friend from near the door. He's holding a cup of coffee in each hand. He smiles at me and raises an eyebrow at his friend. "Ready to go?"

The mysterious stranger jerks his chin as if to say, *Give me a minute*, and his friend shrugs.

When he looks back down at me, my heart just about pounds right out of my damn chest. I'm frozen, waiting to see what he'll do.

Is he going to touch me? Kiss me? Introduce himself? Give me his phone number?

Nothing. The seconds tick by, and he does nothing. But his smile is growing.

Oh. Ohhhh, shit.

He wants *me* to take the first step. And he doesn't know

that I did exactly that last night—and then I promised Prince I'd wait for him.

Shit. Don't get me wrong, this Daddy is hot. I like him a lot. But I promised Prince I'd wait for him.

Who could believe this is my life? All this time living in my own fantasy world, and I'm suddenly entangled with two hot older men. One brings me to the light, while the other meets me in the dark. Both of them make me feel things I've never felt before. And none of us know each other's names.

I have to find a way to let him down, and quickly. So I call up the memory of Prince's hand on my back, his lips on the side of my neck, his gentle touch as he tucked me in last night… and, at last, I tear my gaze away and stare down at my homework.

"Anyway," I mumble, trying to act like my heart isn't leaping out of my mouth. "Thanks. I'll see you around, yeah?"

Damn it. I couldn't be less graceful if I tried. I hope that didn't hurt his feelings.

But the Daddy just smiles crookedly, like he was expecting it, and heads for the door. "See you around, Beauty."

The Daddy strides right out of the shop, grabbing his coffee from his friend along the way. Just before the door closes, he breaks into a cheery little whistle that catches me by surprise.

The second the coffee shop door swings closed and his whistle fades away, the table breaks out in chaos.

"You're into Daddies?" Robby's jaw drops. "You? Daddies?"

"Jesus, Briar!" Kurt laughs. "You kept that a secret."

"I told you guys he'd be into *something!*" Theo exclaims.

"Dude, dude," Robby says, gently shaking me by the

shoulder. "Tell me you already got his number and you didn't just blank him."

I grab his arm before he can get up to chase after the guy on my behalf. "No. But it's okay," I promise him, and his eyebrows fly up almost into his hairline. "Really," I add, laughing at the confusion on his face.

Robby slowly sinks into his chair again. "So what the hell *was* all of that?"

Like I know.

Under the weight of their expectant stares, all I can do is shrug. "Maybe a sign?" I grin sheepishly, reaching down to fidget with the pages of my textbooks. "Or maybe it's just confirmation bias."

Everyone snorts with laughter, and Robby rolls his eyes. "Well, that *is* a sign of something. Maybe you won't fail the test."

My heart lurches as I press my palms together. "From your lips to—"

"—Daddy's dick?" Theo interrupts, ducking as I threaten to throw a fistful of napkins at him.

Everyone's laughing, and I just know they're never going to let me live this down… but at least my big secret is still safe.

What they don't know—or hear creeping into my room late at night—won't hurt anyone.

CHAPTER

Ten

BRIAR

WHEN THE HELL IS MY PRINCE GOING TO COME?

There's lots of reasons I want to know. But right now, one of them feels bigger—and harder—than the rest of them.

It's been two long nights without jerking off. I can barely believe how much self-restraint I've had. Not even a little tug while I'm shaking it in the bathroom, or a fondle while getting dressed. There were moments I thought I'd give in, but I didn't. I'm not going to break my Prince's rule. Not even if my balls turn blue.

I just want to know how much longer I have to wait for him.

"This is the hardest thing I've ever done," I mumble, rolling onto my back. I wait for the prickle of desire to subside as all my blood rushes south. Now the sheets are softly teasing my midnight wood… but if I lie on my front, I'll just end up grinding against the bed.

Come on. Think about Prince Charming.

Not that I need any encouragement. I've been thinking about him almost every minute of the day. Whether I'm in class or cleaning the house, I can't stop remembering the warm pressure of Prince's hand against my hip, or the fullness of his cock driving deep into my ass.

And now, he's the face of all my fantasies.

They sound like him—his warm, husky voice and effortlessly commanding presence. They smell, taste, *feel* like him. When I imagine a strong chest pressed up against my naked back, it's his.

I'm his.

If he wants me.

No. I can't start thinking like that. I shove my arms above my head, spreading my legs like a starfish. *Prince will come*, I repeat my mantra, sucking in my breath and letting it as slow as I can. *Prince will come... Prince will come... Prince will—wait. What was that?*

I swear I just heard the window frame creak.

My eyes want to fly open. I squeeze them shut as hard as I can, listening so intently that I can barely breathe.

There it is—that distinctive smell of sweat, cologne, citrus, and leather. A footstep scuffs against the floor.

He's back!

Anticipation burns through me like a lightning strike. My throat is tight, and my hard-on strains to lift the sheets even further.

There's no chance I can hide how awake and needy I am in the moonlight. It's almost impossible to breathe at all, let alone deep or evenly.

Another step scuffs against the floor, much closer to the bed.

Shit.

I manage not to squeak with anticipation, but I think I flinched.

I try to hide it by stirring a little bit and sighing. I keep my eyes closed as I turn my head to the left against the pillow, nestling my cheek into my bicep.

Prince doesn't say a word, but there's a soft puff of air from nearby—a chuckle.

There's footsteps again. Slow and deliberate, as Prince walks around to the other side of the bed.

The mattress creaks slightly under his weight.

Breathe in, breathe out, stay still.

My whole body is alight with white-hot, eager fire. I'm going out of my mind, I'm so turned on and ready for whatever the hell he's going to do.

He's close. The bed shifts under his weight, like he's crawling toward me. I can hear his breathing now, and his scent fills my nostrils.

Oh, fuck.

I hear the *snick-snick-snick* sound of a zipper sliding down, slower than anyone in the world has ever unzipped anything.

Prince Charming loves teasing the ever-loving fuck out of me while I can't do a thing. And it's working. My cock is so rock-hard that the flushed, throbbing head is leaking precum.

I swear, if he starts outright talking dirty, teasing me about secretly being awake… I'll probably cum hands-free.

But he doesn't. He stays tortuously silent, letting me have my make-believe—making me commit to it. I have to keep showing my Prince my deepest, filthiest desires.

Oh, fuck.

Prince's weight settles on either side of my head as he straddles my chest. His thumb brushes against the corner of my jaw, so softly I could almost think I was imagining it.

My lips part as I turn my head toward him, drawing rough, uneven breaths.

I can tell from the musky scent that his cock is just above my face. And I'd do anything to have it in my mouth right *the fuck* now.

I won't be able to pretend for much longer before I start to moan and beg, and I really want him to get to the action first.

That's the hottest part of all—finding myself already in the middle of fulfilling his desires.

Although my hard-on betrays me on that front. It's twitching and helplessly leaking straight through the sheet.

Please please let me taste you now before I go out of my mind, please...!

Prince's thumb traces along my jaw, still ghosting gently across my skin, and rests on my lower lip.

And then he pulls his hand away, and something else replaces it. Something a *lot* harder and thicker. But he isn't pushing forward yet, or settling his weight on my chest to pin me down.

He's staying where he is, enjoying my first reaction. My tongue runs clumsily across and around the hard, mushroom-shaped tip of his dick.

Prince tickles me under my chin, and I automatically close my lips around it.

Oh, fuck. Oh, god, it's hard to breathe this way… but it's so much hotter. The only thing I can smell or taste is *him*, crouching so carefully over me.

Then Prince jerks his hips forward, sliding into the back of my mouth without hesitation. He starts moving, slow and steady, one hand settling on my hair to hold me gently in place.

Not that I have any choice, with the hard length of him forcing my head to stay exactly where it is.

Prince's shaft is velvety, rock-hard in my mouth, and so thick I feel like I'm about to choke. He pushes further and further into my mouth until the head of his cock slides right into my throat.

"Nnnh... nnngh...!" I choke out softly, struggling for breath.

Fuck. My head is spinning for dear life. He pulls back, and I can't help suspecting that he's about to—

Oh fuck fuck *fuuuuck*!

Prince shoves himself all the way to the back of my throat. He's face-fucking me slowly, but I can't pretend to ignore it any longer.

I'm choking on the thick length he's pushing into my throat, burning up with arousal until I can't stay still.

"Mmnh...!" I squeak softly as my fingers curl into tight fists.

Prince gives the hottest fucking laugh I've *ever* heard in my goddamn life—deep and rough and dark.

"Hello again, Beauty," he breathes out through the darkness. He pulls back and slams into the back of my throat again as he growls, "Now, suck on your Prince's dick."

I choke and squeal, arching against him. A flush races from my cheeks straight down my body as my hard-on throbs with desperation.

The moment I pull my hands free, Prince grabs them and yanks them over my head, sliding his fingers between mine.

I can't get away. He's got me trapped and helpless, exactly like I wanted.

"Mmnh!" I squeak as loud as I can, my voice muffled around his shaft.

"I'm sorry to disturb your sweet dreams," Prince whispers. "But I'll make sure you sleep soundly until dawn. Would you like that, Beauty?"

My cock throbs for dear life as he pumps his hips slowly and steadily. I might cum just from the friction against the damp sheet.

My mouth is a little too full to answer, so I shake my head slightly. I can't even pretend to beg, though. I'm dying to hear what filthy promises he'll make next.

Prince laughs roughly and leans forward. "Don't worry, Beauty. I won't be telling you a sweet fairytale." He spreads his knees and digs his nails into my scalp, ignoring my whimpers. "It's too late at night for *that* kind of story. Only the bad men and the beasts are up this late."

Jesus. Fucking. Christ.

It's all I can do to hold myself back as Prince throws back his head and groans.

"Mmffngh!" I whimper. I can't form words around the hard dick filling up my mouth. His balls slap my chin with every thrust.

Prince just pounds my throat harder and faster. Every time I try to arch off the bed, he pushes harder into me until I collapse into it again, and then he moans in satisfaction.

"I thought you didn't want to talk, Beauty," Prince Charming taunts me.

Oh, that's really not fair. Damn it. Why do I love it so much?

I blush furiously, but I can't stop the soft, embarrassed noise that escapes.

Prince laughs, slowing his pace enough to pin both my wrists in one hand. Then, he rakes his fingers back through my hair. "I saw you in the moonlight, like my secret treasure.

Aching… hard… desperate. With lips like those, you were made to be my happy ending."

I quiver from head to toe. Every muscle is drawing tight.

Fuck. After months of stroking myself as hard and fast as I can, I'm about to cum from the sheets brushing across me…

And from being my Prince's secret treasure.

I squeak shyly, squeezing my eyes shut as my body quivers and clenches tight.

Prince leans down to growl into my ear, grunting with each thrust. "A real prince knows—*nnngh!*—his Beauty—*hnnh!*—craves—the—beast!"

Oh fuuuuck—I'm so fucking close…!

"Yesyesyes… yes!" Prince grabs my hair even tighter until my scalp burns, ignoring my feeble protests and forcing my lips to the very base of his shaft.

Then his rhythm breaks.

Prince arches, goes still for a moment, and his hips jerk forward. He's swelling, squirting his thick, salty load across my tongue and straight to the back of my throat.

His groan rings through the room. And all I can do is gulp, swallowing again and again as he takes his sweet time to drain himself dry in my mouth.

I'm burning up with need, more desperate than I've been in my entire life to touch myself. And he's not in any rush to let go of my wrists, however much I tug at them.

I need to touch myself! Need it, need it, need it so bad!

"Please," I try to moan around his cock, but my mouth is still too full to form the word.

But finally, Prince lets go of my hair and the prickling eases in my scalp. As he slides out of my mouth, he reaches back and pushes a hand under the sheet behind himself.

Fingers close tightly around my aching shaft, and my whole body explodes with heat.

"Nnnh!" I almost buck right off the bed, my lips parting as I gasp and squirm underneath him. It's almost too much sensation, but I'm *seconds* away at most…

Prince strokes me once, twice—and I'm lost in ecstasy.

Yes…! Fuck, oh my fucking—

I can't stop shuddering, head to toe. Every muscle twangs with desperate release.

I buck wildly into his hand, gasping as I spill my hot juices all over his hand, my stomach, the sheets…

Time disappears, and the world goes black.

The next thing I know, I'm no longer under the sheets. I don't feel his weight on my chest. But there's still a thick, warm blanket of satisfaction wrapped tightly around my bones.

"Mmmm," I moan softly, trying to push past the sleepiness.

"A happy ending worth waiting for?" Prince murmurs from near my ear. He's sitting by my head now, one hand gently stroking through my hair.

It feels so sweet and gentle.

How much time passed? I have no idea. But I can't remember the last time I came like that… if ever.

I want to say *yes*, or *thank you*, or *I needed you*. All I can manage is a soft, "Gnnngh," and a quiver of pleasure.

He chuckles deeply, and I suddenly realize what disturbed me from the blissful blackness. Prince just finished wiping me clean with tissues. He tugs the sheet across me, helping find a dry spot for me to sleep under.

I giggle sheepishly. "There…" I swallow my clumsy

tongue and try again. "There was... a lot stored up," I mumble.

He snorts. "There sure was, Beauty." Soft, warm lips press against my forehead and I smile. "You listened to my rules," he murmurs, sounding surprised. "You... you waited for me."

Of course I did!

But I can't possibly find the words to explain how long I've waited for a firm hand—for *his* firm hand. All I can manage is a breathless laugh and a little nod.

Then I bite my lip. "And... and you came," I murmur, probably sounding as surprised as he did a moment ago.

Prince's hand tightens in my hair for a moment, and then he rubs my scalp gently with his fingertips. "Yeah. What was it like, waiting?"

"Good," I beam, nuzzling my cheek into the pillow as I beam toward him. "I mean, agony. But a good kind."

Prince cups my cheek, and then he leans down to press his lips slowly and gently against mine.

Oh, holy crap.

I've never been kissed like this before. Slowly, like there's all the time in the world, but full of more desire than I can possibly imagine.

And promises. There are promises in his lips, somehow transmitted to mine without any need for words. I understand them all.

It feels too good to be true, but I couldn't possibly imagine the soft taste of his lips.

Not even in my wildest dreams.

At last, Prince pulls back and rests his forehead against mine.

"You haven't opened your eyes once." His words come in short, warm puffs of air that tickle my sensitive lips.

I gulp for breath. "Mmhmm."

Something is surging between us—something I don't understand. Part of me wants to look at him, to see for myself who he is. Whether I'm feeling what I think I am.

But I'm afraid it'll shatter this perfect fantasy.

"It's… um… it's hotter that way?" My voice trails off as my cheeks burn.

Ugh. Even I'm not convinced by that answer.

He huffs softly. "And the real reason?"

I don't know how to say it. But Prince gives me time to think about it. He just waits, quiet and patient and still.

Shit.

I've been waiting so long for my prince that I never thought about what to do when he came. I guess it's time to be honest with him—and with myself.

CHAPTER
Eleven

BRIAR

I don't know what to tell Prince.

He hasn't given me a reason not to trust him... but I'm not sure if I trust my own judgment. Any sane person would look at everything I've done over this past week and say *no*. Probably with several more expletives. But if I hadn't done any of it, we wouldn't be here.

I'm afraid to fill the comfortable night air between us... but I guess I could start there.

"It scares me," I murmur softly. "Knowing who you are underneath first. And knowing that *you* know me the same way." Then I furrow my eyebrows. "If you get what I mean."

"Yes," Prince says softly. "There's the knowing that comes with seeing someone in the light... and the knowing of seeing what's inside them, and helping bring those things to life."

"Like what?" I murmur. It's not just an excuse to hear him talk, either. What he's saying makes sense.

"Seeing their deepest, most shameful fantasies. Understanding something about them that they might not have admitted even to themselves. Liking them, even growing to love them, despite... no, not despite it. *Because* of it, and everything you understand about them through it."

Whoa. Did I hear that right?

Is he trying to tell me that he... he might just grow to love me?

My gulp sounds even louder in the darkness. "What does it say about me, then?"

He reaches out and rests a hand on my shoulder. "You obviously want to hide from the light—from seeing and making a choice for yourself. But you're desperate to be seen."

Oh my god, kill me now.

I dramatically roll onto my front, hiding my face in the pillow.

Prince laughs softly and rests a hand on my back. "Did you hear me when I said I like you because of it?"

I blush furiously, but there's something warm and soft exploding in my chest. Gradually, I let go of the pillow and turn my cheek against it so I can shake my head. "Yeah. But it's hard to trust I won't get burned in the light."

A breath rushes out, like I just kicked Prince in the chest.

For once, he doesn't have an answer ready to go.

The seconds are ticking by, and still nothing. Maybe I hit a nerve. God, what if he likes hiding behind masks because he had a terrible encounter with a chandelier or something?

Just before I can burst out with inappropriate questions, Prince sighs. "I understand. Deep down, we're all afraid of the light. But we need it. We want to know and be known."

There's an intense sadness—even loneliness—ringing clear as a bell in his voice. And even with my eyes closed, I can't hold back the tears.

We've both been hiding in the shadows, haven't we?

He's so confident that I didn't imagine he could be just as afraid as me. But I guess he needed the darkness too, to let his desires be known.

"Oh, sweetheart," Prince murmurs. "Come here." The bed shifts behind me as he stretches out along the bed and slides his arm over my waist. Gently, he pulls my back against his chest.

I sniffle into my pillow as he wraps himself around me. He's the perfect size to wrap me up in his strong arms. I never imagined him holding me like this—my shoulder blades against his chest, his lips against the back of my neck, rubbing my chest in gentle little circles.

He holds me softly for as long as I need to cry, and then for a little while after the tears dry up.

Finally, I clear my throat a few times.

"Why'd you wait so long to come?"

"You get more stamina over the years—"

I giggle hoarsely and shove an elbow back into Prince, wiping my arm across my eyes. "Come *here*, I mean," I laugh, trying to keep my voice down.

Prince chuckles softly. "I work in, er…" he pauses like he's choosing his words carefully before he says, "hospitality."

Bartender? Bouncer? Stripper? A few options automatically present themselves, and they all come with visuals I *really* enjoy.

"My shifts end late." He slowly lets go of me and sits up, gently tucking the covers around my shoulders again. "But that's boring stuff."

"Good," I whisper, snuggling into the affectionate touch. I don't want this moment to be over. "I want to get to know you. And if it's boring, it'll just help me drift off. Win-win."

"Mmm," Prince hums. He runs a hand down my arm,

through the covers, and I smile at the heaviness suddenly in my eyelids. It doesn't take as much work to keep them closed. "I have two jobs. I've spent a long time trying to break into the one I want to do. There's this thing on Friday..." he trails off, his grip tightening on my shoulder.

Holy shit, is he actually nervous?

It makes my heart swell with warmth—and a little bit of pride—that Prince trusts me enough to show me this side of him. "Oh? A big break?"

"Yeah. *The* big break. This industry is like a castle, and... I wasn't born with the key." Prince sighs. "Some days, I wonder if I belong in it at all."

Prince's Daddy mask is slipping into something a little more natural as he speaks. The warm, sultry voice has turned more rough and gruff, but it still sounds comfortably familiar.

It makes me trust him.

"You got in here," I yawn softly.

Prince pauses and then huffs a soft laugh. "That's because you leave the window open, my dear," he says drily.

I giggle. "Every castle has an open window. You can find it. Prince Charming is good at that stuff."

Prince chuckles and leans over me to cup my cheek in his palm. "As long as there's a Beauty waiting for me on the other side."

"I—I know what you mean," I mumble, stifling a yawn as he runs his hand gently to my shoulder again. "I feel like I've been following other people's dreams."

"What makes you say that?"

"I'm supposed to be going into my last year of college." I sigh. "Assuming I pass summer classes. And then I don't know what I'll do. No grad school wants a psych major who was too busy jerking off to learn anything."

Prince hums under his breath. "You started getting these uncontrollable urges, and it began impacting your life?"

"Yes—" I break off, because something's gnawing at the back of my mind. "Wait, no. It was the night after I failed my first test, when I woke up and discovered... well, all of this."

I can't believe I forgot that. For months, I've been telling myself that it's the other way around... beating myself up for being such a loser.

Prince hums and nods. "But waking up in the middle of the night can't be helpful, either."

I nod slowly, my cheeks burning. "Yeah. No matter how sleep-deprived I am, no matter how bad I'm doing at classes... I haven't been able to stop myself. Until now. These last two nights."

"What's changed?" I snort, but before I can be sassy, Prince gently flicks my shoulder. "Besides me."

I dunno. It's easier to follow someone else's rules than my own? I shrug. "I had something to look forward to?"

Prince doesn't say anything. He just runs his hand gently from my shoulder down my arm until he's stroking the back of my hand.

"Which I haven't had in... a long time now." I frown into the darkness. "I come from the kind of family where nobody expected me to achieve much. I was just supposed to look pretty, follow the path, go to the right school... graduate with a degree, any degree. The only reason I'm majoring in psychology is because my friends are. But none of it is for *me*."

Prince still says nothing, but my chest aches.

"I'm just… an empty vessel for everyone else to pour their desires into. Like Sleeping Beauty."

I can't believe I said it out loud. But at the same time, I can. I feel so damn safe with my Prince Charming… and it's not just because I don't have to see his face when I'm talking. It's about who he is.

"But you're not," Prince says softly. He gently pulls his hand out from between my palms, tangling his fingers in my hair to rub slow circles against my scalp.

I snort. "But I am. Look at me."

"I am looking at you," Prince reminds me softly. "And listening. Sometimes you don't quite know how, but you've already shown and told me who you are. And that's the one thing Sleeping Beauty doesn't do."

A second ago, I was all ready for a fight. Now I'm just frowning into the darkness, my lips slowly parting.

"Huh?" I finally manage.

Prince chuckles softly. "Why does it appeal to you so much, having me stumble upon you? Why is it hotter for you to pretend to be asleep?"

My cheeks burn. I've never thought that much about it. At least, not without judging myself. "Um… it just is?"

Prince huffs softly. "Try again."

I grimace, squirming with embarrassment, but he just waits patiently until I finally manage to say it out loud. "I never have to say what I want. I don't even have to *know* what I want. I can just be…"

"An empty vessel," he echoes my words from just a minute ago, and then he kisses the back of my neck. "A toy for princes and beasts to play with."

My breath catches in my throat, and my eyes fly open as I stare ahead of me into the darkness.

Fuck. He's right.

I groan, rolling over until I'm face-down in the pillows. "Is that a bad thing?"

"That you want to be helpless?" I nod, and Prince presses his lips softly against the back of my neck. "No, sweetheart. Admitting what you want makes you a stronger man… and a very good boy."

A good boy? Holy shit. Maybe Prince Charming could be everything I've ever wanted, all at once: a brave prince, a wicked beast… *and* a wise Daddy.

"I'm not saying *not* to let yourself be an empty vessel," he purrs, warm and sultry again. "I, for one, enjoy it."

My throat is tight, but I can't help a soft squeak.

Prince chuckles. "Just do it on purpose. Live your dreams at night, and you'll have more room to discover what your dreams are during the day."

That sounds… that sounds really nice.

Shit. I'm sleepy again. I can't hold back another huge yawn.

"And before any of that, you clearly need to sleep," Prince murmurs, pushing himself to his feet.

"Wait," I whisper. "Will you come back on Friday?" I lick my lips nervously, and it takes everything I have to force out another word. "Please?"

What if he says no? What if he doesn't want me that often? Or ever again?

This. Is. The. *Worst.*

In the darkness, I don't have a clue what he's thinking. My whole kink is sitting and stewing and waiting… but I can't stand another second.

"I know that's the night of your big break. But you could come before…? Or after, and tell me how it went…? My roommates always go out early for pre-drinks. And they'll be out all night. So basically, come anytime. I'll be in bed—"

Prince takes hold of both my shoulders, gently rolling me onto my back, and then he kisses me.

Ohhhh. Oh, fuck.

This kiss tells me more than a thousand words, or a hundred lingering stares. It's a promise that blows away all my worries like dust in the wind.

It says: *Whenever you need me, I'll be here.*

Prince's mouth slides softly across mine, gentle yet demanding. He sucks my lower lip until I melt into a thousand little puddles of goo, and then he pushes his tongue between my lips to utterly claim me. *Every* part of me, whether it lives in the shadows or the light.

"I'll come," Prince promises in a whisper against my lips as he finally pulls away. "And you really are a fast learner, Beauty. I hope you remember that now."

I swallow hard.

I can't get over the way he sees all of me. And he might even grow to love it, in time. As long as I let him in… through more than just the window.

Maybe even the front door.

"There's a lockbox outside," I whisper, my heart fluttering nervously. "You've slain enough dragons to have the castle keys. The code's 6969."

Prince's breath catches. There's a few long seconds of silence, and then he snorts.

"6969? That's a terrible code." Despite the dry tone in his voice, Prince puts his hand on my shoulder for a quick squeeze… like he wants me to know how touched he is.

I giggle as I nuzzle into my pillow. "But you won't forget it. That makes it a great code."

"And it's easy for anyone to guess, which makes it—"

"A great code, if you have *my* kink."

Prince gives up and huffs a soft laugh. "Are you a beauty *and* a brat?"

"I don't—" I yawn again. "Mmmnh. I dunno, remember? You'll have to find out."

"Oh, I will," he promises in that warm, raspy whisper that turns me on so much. "But first, you sleep."

That's one command I'm happy to obey.

Just as the blackness tugs at me, I hear Prince's voice one more time. "Beauty?"

"Mmm?"

"I'm proud of you."

That's it. That's all I've ever wanted to hear.

Any tension I had left—hell, any tension I *ever* had—melts away. I can't manage words, but a soft, happy moan slips free.

"Sweet dreams, Beauty."

Maybe my life is the good kind of fairytale after all… and it'll have the kind of ending I've always wanted.

CHAPTER

Twelve

BRIAR

I'M PROUD OF MYSELF.

My roommates left an hour ago for pre-drinks and the Vibes party, and I'm exactly where I want to be.

And this time, I told them. No more *maybe* or *ummm* or *we'll see*. Just *I don't want to come tonight*. Which is only true for one of the definitions of the word *come*… but they don't need to know that.

Despite the rain outside, my window is cracked open enough to be pushed the rest of the way. And I left my bedroom door unlocked, too. That way, Prince has his choice of entrances… so to speak.

Thump.

The front door slams open and hits the other side of my bedroom wall. My whole body twitches with surprise like a fish marooned on the rocks, and then I catch myself.

Damn it, I'm supposed to be asleep!

I collapse into the pillows again, flailing around as I try to artfully-yet-casually arrange all my limbs on the mattress.

"Briiiiiar!"

My heart instantly sinks.

Shit. That's not Prince. It's Robby, and he's hollering at the top of his lungs, hammering on my bedroom door.

"Hey, old man! Wake up!"

Shit. Did something happen at the bar? "What? Give me a second!" I call back, worry rising in my throat as I scramble to find my boxers.

It's only been an hour. What the hell could have happened for him to come back? For me, of all people? Among the many other things I'm *not*: a first aider, legal expert, or bondage professional.

I'm just tugging my waistband into place when I hear laughter echo in the front hall.

"Assholes," I grumble, marching for my bedroom door. I can't believe I was actually worried for a second. They'd better have a good reason for interrupting my private time—er, I mean, *sleep*—tonight, of all nights.

I wanted everything perfect and ready for Prince... including me. And thanks to these dumbasses, my hard-on has basically fled to start a new life abroad.

"You'll wanna hear this—"

"Hear what?" I demand, yanking open the door. I'd like to think I'm glaring at them, but I'm really just blinking like an owl into the blinding hallway light.

"This!" Robby shoves something into my hand. They're suddenly all quiet—or as quiet as they can be when the air is crackling with excitement.

"It better be a winning lottery ticket," I grumble as I squint down at the paper in my hand. It's a flyer for tonight's party—and it's weirdly sticky.

"Ew!" I shove it back at Robby. "Has this been spunked on?"

"No, dumbass. It's ice cream."

"And that isn't a euphemism for a Canadian's cumshot," Robby cheerfully clarifies. "But no—look!" He jabs a finger at the photo in the middle of it.

I roll my eyes, look down, and…

My heart just stopped.

Shit.

No. No way. I feel like I've seen a ghost.

I rip the flyer right out of Robby's hands to look closer. I want to shake my head, but I'm almost frozen to the spot.

I know the man looking up from behind a DJ deck like he's irritated by the camera's presence.

The headliner tonight is none other than the Daddy-turned-wicked fairy. And pushed up on his forehead so he can see is a feathered red-and-black mask.

His name is DJ Prince. As in… *my* Prince.

"Holy shit," I breathe out.

My friends are all waving their hands and talking at the same time, but I can't pick out voices over the thunder of my heartbeat in my own ears. And I feel like I just got hit by a freight train.

All along, it was the same guy? I should have known. It was too much of a coincidence.

I just didn't want to see it. But it makes sense.

That's why he didn't want me to see him in the light. *That's* why he picked me, of all people, to stop and talk to that first night we met.

Is this supposed to be a punishment for how we treated him? Am I just some kind of joke to him, or a game?

My friends are slowly realizing something is wrong. They're elbowing each other, hissing under their breath until they're all just silently staring at me.

"Briar...?" Robby's brows furrow in confusion. "We—We thought you wanted to talk to him...?"

I do. I mean... I *did*. A few days ago, I would have jumped for joy and kissed them all.

But now...

Now, I feel like I've given so much of myself—my innocence, my desire, my heart—to a man who was laughing at me all along.

"What—" Robby whirls around, and then I hear it too.

There's a noise outside. The front door handle is rattling softly, like someone's just put a key into the lock.

All my roommates are staring at the front door. I'm frozen in my bedroom doorway, the only one who knows who's there.

Prince is about to step right into the light.

I'm so fucking scared that I'm right about this. I'm scared that the truth that's about to be exposed will break the fairytale spell between us—and break my heart.

But it's too late to change course.

The door opens, and here he is.

The Prince who stepped through my window and into all my daydreams... even the soft, tender ones I barely hoped for.

He's standing at my front door, illuminated by the beam of light that spills out into the evening. And he's even wearing that same fucking red and black feathered mask.

"You?" Robby exclaims. "What the hell?"

Prince stops in his tracks, clearly taken by surprise. Behind the mask, his eyes dart between all my roommates... and then they land on me.

I recognize those stormy gray eyes now—the slope of his shoulders, the smell of his cologne, all of it.

His eyes soften as soon as he sees me, but my jaw is just growing tighter and tighter.

Prince looks down at the flyer in my hand. His lips slowly part, his shoulders go stiff, and he looks back up at me like a cornered animal.

"Tell me I'm fucking wrong," I breathe out.

Was it a prince or a wicked fairy sneaking through my window, whispering sweet promises in the dark?

I don't even know if there's a difference anymore.

"DJ Prince," Jeff murmurs as my roommates start to put together the pieces. "You're that guy from the bar? And the coffee shop?"

With one shaking hand, Prince pushes the mask up and off to sit on top of his head. "I am," he says, talking to them but looking at me.

"Jesus Christ." My whole body seems to collapse as I sag against the door frame. "Fuck. Fuck, fuck, *fuck*."

The sweet-tongued prince who came for me in the dark *is* the prickly Daddy who came for me in the light.

At least I know why I liked them both so much. Because I was falling for the same man all along… and he knew it.

He just didn't want me to know.

"*Fuck*," I breathe out, and Prince still says nothing, just watches me with that guilty look.

My heart twists so sharply that I think it might have just snapped in two. My hand flies up to my chest like I'm suddenly trying to keep all the pieces of my heart in place.

As Robby draws himself up to his full height, he turns up the volume on his voice. "What the fuck are you doing in our *house*? Are you stalking him?! I swear—"

"I-I can explain," Prince murmurs, holding up a hand. "But you might want to hear it from him first."

Suddenly everyone turns, staring at *me* for some explanation, when it was Prince who knew what the fuck he was doing all along.

Prince stares pleadingly at me, but I shake my head slowly.

"N-No," I breathe out, my throat seizing up.

I don't even know what I'm saying no to.

No, this can't be true? No, I don't want to give you another chance? No, I'm not going to explain why you had the lockbox code for our house?

Or… all of the above?

It hurts like hell to see the look on his face—a look that tells me he knew damn well that he wasn't acting like the hero of my story. Despite all his pretty words, *he* was the one keeping me in the dark.

Robby huffs, glaring and bristling at Prince like a wild boar prepared to charge. "Briar?" he asks.

Fuck. Now he knows my name. But I guess it's too late anyway.

My eyes are still locked on Prince. The world is going blurry with tears, but I still can't miss the movement of his soft lips forming the shape of my name… mouthing it like a prayer.

I don't want to hear him say it out loud. It would hurt too much.

"Get out," I breathe out.

My hands are curled into fists all of a sudden, my whole body stiff with outrage and disappointment and fear.

And a bone-deep humiliation that, for the first time, *doesn't* feel good.

"But—"

"Get *out*," I snap, so loudly that even Robby jumps. "Now!"

Prince's face crumples.

That look makes my heart explode into even tinier fragments, and I wish it didn't. I wish I could just be so pissed at him that nothing he says or does can slip in past my defenses and touch me again.

But I feel his pain on top of my own, and I can't stop the tears spilling from my eyes, running down my cheeks.

Prince stumbles backward off the step. He takes another pace back toward the gate, still staring like he can't quite believe what he's hearing. Like he's hoping I'm about to change my mind.

I shake my head.

Prince's shoulders crumple. He tears his gaze away from mine, whirls on his heel, and shoves his way back through the gate to vanish into the night.

"And don't you ever try and sneak back in here!" Robby hollers after him, stomping to the gate and shielding his eyes against the rain to watch him go.

Then he storms back in and slams the door.

I'm still blinking back my tears, but suddenly I'm being steered to the living room, pressed into a chair, handed a mug of hot chocolate.

Someone's telling me to drink up so I don't go into shock. I nod automatically and sip, still staring into space.

I'm gradually becoming aware that my friends are all talking over each other in a clamor of voices.

"What the hell is going on?"

"He's fucking stalking Briar, dude. I can't believe it!"

"I can. I knew he was up to no good."

"How'd he get the code?"

"Should we report him?"

"Who used the lockbox last? Did they scramble it afterwards?"

My head is whirling.

No. No, I'm not doing this again—going along with everything.

I suck in a quick breath and set down my drink. "Wait."

Kurt glances at me, then nudges Robby, who's talking loudly about a video doorbell.

I'm going to have to speak up if I want to be heard.

The Prince I've always dreamed of... if he ever existed... he'd be proud of me for doing this.

That hurts even more. I swallow hard and curl my hands into fists again as my throat goes tihgt.

The old Briar would have just let them keep talking, so long as I never had to think about it again.

But I'm not that guy anymore.

Of course I'm nervous about it. I'm not busting at the seams to admit that Prince has been sneaking through my open window to ravish me while they all thought I was having wholesome early nights in bed.

But a wise Daddy—or a wicked fairy, or just a cruel prince—once told me that everyone wants to know and be known.

I'm not just a vessel for him, or for anyone else. I have dreams of my own. Some of which happen to be pretty fucking filthy... and I'm trying to be proud of that.

That means waking up and learning how to let people in through the front door.

"Wait!"

Silence falls as everyone stares at me. I gulp another mouthful of hot chocolate for fortitude, and then I draw a breath.

"There's something I haven't told you."

CHAPTER
Thirteen

PRINCE

I'M GONNA THROTTLE DARREN.

Sure, Quarrel prodded me into calling Vibes' manager after we ran into Beauty in the coffee shop. And I was the one who worked my magic to get myself top billing. But Darren put my face on the freaking flyer without even asking me.

Yeah, that's how promoting works. I know, I know. I just want an excuse to be mad at someone other than myself.

My love life is a disaster. If I crash and burn tonight, that's it for my career, too. And all of it will be my own damn fault.

Fuck, fuck, fuck. At least the weather fits the mood. It's raining so hard that my jacket is already soaked through.

Briar.

It's such a beautiful name, but I can't bring myself to think of him as anything but Beauty. *My* Beauty.

All I wanted was to sit and talk with him in the dark, where I'm safest. Where I was starting to believe that I could be cared for, even wanted, once I finally stepped into the light.

Of course I've been worried that he'd react this way. I've spent my life with my guard up and my heart behind a wall, expecting to disappoint people. But the way we were getting to know each other in the night…

For a moment, I dared to hope that this time, it would be different in the daylight. It felt too perfect, the way he called me Prince without even knowing who I am. Like it was meant to be.

I'm effortlessly confident when I'm around Beauty, and he responds so well to it. Bringing out his true nature is as easy as breathing. His desire to be helpless makes it obvious to us both that he isn't.

I was starting to feel like I could be the prince in his story and not the wicked fairy after all. But I was too selfish—and, under all my bravery, too afraid—to tell him who I really am.

Of course I *wanted* to. I wanted him to know why he felt so safe with me—why it wasn't so crazy after all, the two of us falling for each other. I wanted him to be *happy* that I was his Prince Charming.

I just… wanted Beauty to want me.

That's not a good enough excuse for what I did. I just wish I could tell him I wasn't playing games—that I wanted him to see me as much as I loved to see him.

I don't think he has the slightest idea how special he is. There's nobody else quite like him. Even Sleeping Beauty is destined to be a queen. And I know my Beauty is destined to do big things, too. I just wanted to be up close to watch him blossom.

Truth be told, I think I've been falling for Beauty since the first time we met. But now that he knows who I am, he hates me.

Feels like my chest is about to break open and spill my guts right onto the sidewalk.

The truth fucking hurts.

As I duck under the awning at Vibes, my eyes land on the stupid poster plastered all over their front door, mocking me —my own face with my mask up on my forehead, the way it is right now.

I guess a mask can do one of two things. It can help me be myself... or it can help me be someone else when being myself hurts too much. For tonight, I can put on my mask and pretend to be okay.

And then I'll figure out how to rip out my broken heart and put it somewhere it'll never hurt me again.

Fourteen

BRIAR

I can't believe I'm doing this.

"Are you sure this is enough to get me in?"

We're all huddled together in the lineup for Vibes. Two of my friends are holding umbrellas, trying to keep the rain from dribbling down between them, but it's a losing battle.

My friends are all in elaborate latex and leather and kinky stuff, and I feel like I'm showing up for a costume party.

"You're fine. Leave it alone," Robby tells me, smacking my fingers away before I can tug at the shoulder of my white toga. "Just look what everyone else is wearing."

I see partygoers who clearly understood the assignment, and others who just wore the same old stuff they always wear. I'll fit right in wearing Robby's toga, along with Jeff's lace-up gold boots and harness, and a feathered gold mask that Theo mysteriously found after last week's party.

"I'm not wearing anything underneath. That's kinky, right?" I quip, and they all crack up laughing.

It was sweet how fast they whipped up an outfit for me,

the moment I told them I wanted to come with them. And I'm just surprised that I finally feel good coming out.

Maybe it's because, at last, they all know… and nothing's different.

I mean, they obviously teased me for being a freak. But no more or less than they all tease each other. It's nice to finally be included. I didn't realize how much time I've spent silently fretting that maybe I'm the *real* freak here.

Maybe our freak flags are a little different, but I'm not alone with it anymore.

There's his face again. The closer we get, the more copies of Prince Charming's face I see. The posters are plastered all over the windows, until it looks like he's staring at me with irritation from every which way.

I'm still not sure how I feel… but at least I know what I want.

I had to come out tonight to see Prince in his element… and hopefully talk to him one more time.

Earlier, I didn't act like my best self—like the man Prince has been teaching me to become. I was too lost in my own hurt to realize that, for a second time, I didn't stand up for him, or even for what *I* want.

That's not to say I'm not mad at him. Because I totally am. I don't know why he kept his identity secret from me… but I'm ready to hear his side of the story, too, before I make any hasty decisions.

I don't know if he'll forgive me, or if I'll forgive him, or both.

But I need to see him in the light—even if it's the glare of neon lasers—to understand something about him that I've never gotten to see.

We're at the front of the line now, and everything is a

blur. I hand over my ID and cash, get them back, hold out my arms for the scanner, and laugh nervously as the security guy waves a wand and pretends to sprinkle fairy dust over me.

Then they wave me inside, and my friends point me toward the main room. It's already packed, and I can't help but be happy for Prince. If nothing else, at least tonight *was* the breakout hit he wanted it to be.

"You want company?" Robby leans in to holler at me, and I smile and shake my head. His eyes are already wandering to the darker side rooms.

I cup my hands around my mouth, next to his ear. "I'll be okay. Go have fun."

Robby winks at me and mouths, *You too*. Then my friends melt away into the crowd, and there's only one thing left to do.

I sidle into the room, hugging the wall until I can make out the DJ booth…

There he is. Under the dim lights, on the edge of the crowd, mask pushed up to his forehead again as he looks between the booth and his audience. He's not quite dancing, but he's moving with the crowd.

The closer I get, the more I can see him watching everyone yet no one, utterly in the zone. That must be how he looks when he's with me—responsive to the slightest change in the energy and desires.

That's how he anticipates my needs, like he's reading my mind.

It's one of his gifts—one of many. And I can't shake the feeling that I jumped to conclusions. There's a reason it seemed so unbelievable that he was lying to me, or playing games, or steering me the wrong way.

Because that's not what he meant to do.

I think he just forgot that I'm not a collective entity of an audience to be guided and steered from afar. I'm one person —one scared boy, one Sleeping Beauty who's only just learning how to wake up and go after what I want.

Now I know why I'm here.

I'm here to dance, and study him, and let his spell fall over me once more. From the middle of the dance floor now, there are too many surging bodies for him to know who I am… but I'm close enough to see him, standing alone behind the decks.

How the table turns. Or the turntables.

I just have to pray that afterward—when I approach him —he's ready to let me in.

I don't know how much time has passed. Hours, certainly. I've downed several bottles of water, and turned down quite a few guys hitting on me.

I've already got a date tonight… whether he knows it or not.

He doesn't talk very much during his sets. Whenever he does, his voice is that sultry, dripping-sweet honey I know so well.

And this time, I hear what I've been waiting for. He's thanking everyone, announcing a surprise guest DJ who's taking over the decks until the end of the night… and he's stepping away.

As the track changes and a cheer goes up, I quickly elbow my way through the crowd toward the front. Prince is melting into the shadows against the wall, staring across the crowd with a look I've never seen on his face before.

He looks wired, yet exhausted. He's pouring sweat and

smiling, but there's a sadness in his eyes. I'm just steps away as he slips out from behind the booth, reaching up for the mask like he's considering pulling it back down.

I step out of the shadows and into his path.

God, he's taller than me. I had no idea until now.

Prince sidesteps automatically, nodding politely without looking at me like he's trying to turn me down.

There's no way he'll hear me say anything, this close to the thumping speakers. My heart pounds nervously in my chest as I step again to block his path.

He looks up this time—stares at me, past the flimsy gold mask—and then his jaw drops.

I don't even need to take off my mask. He knows me.

Prince reaches for my hand, and I let him take it to pull me towards the far corner of the room. He effortlessly strides through the crowd, and they just seem to part for him without even knowing they're doing it. It's something about his presence that makes them step aside for him—and me.

That's hot.

With every step, it gets just a little bit quieter. It's still loud by the time we reach the corner, but I don't think either of us can wait long enough to reach somewhere truly quiet.

He spins to face me, his eyes intensely burning with something I can't quite place.

"You came."

I nod as he studies me. He reaches out as if to touch the sweat sheen on my forehead, then hesitates. I bite my lip, nervous all over again as I watch him drop his hand.

"Been here a while?"

I nod again, fumbling with the ribbon at the back of my head until my mask slips off. "I had to see you." I fidget nervously, poking my finger through one of the eyeholes to spin the mask nervously around my hand. "You made me… wake up and open my eyes."

Prince hesitates, watching me with a small, guarded frown. "Did I? Or did I pull the wool over them?"

I wince, but I nod anyway. "Yeah. I know what I want now."

The hope on Prince's face is almost painful to witness. He bites his lip and shoves his hands in his pockets. But even my brave prince can't bring himself to ask. I think he's too afraid of what I might say.

If I didn't already know my answer, that would be my biggest clue… but I think my heart knew all along.

"I want you, Prince. I didn't have to see you to know that. Finding out who you were… it didn't change that."

I can see the breath rushing out of Prince's lungs as his shoulders slump with relief. He reaches out to take my mask from my hand, tucks it into his back pocket… and then he drops to his knees in front of me.

Holy shit.

My cheeks burn as I look around quickly, trying to see who might be watching us. I mean, I didn't think we were done this conversation. And we're right in public! Should we be picking up where we left off—

Prince laughs loudly as he takes both my hands. From the grin on his face, he knows exactly what I was thinking.

Oh. I leapt to conclusions again, didn't I?

"I owe you an apology," Prince tells me, raising his voice and speaking a little slower to make sure I can hear him over the music. His lips pull down into a ragged, sorrowful frown. "Hiding the truth was wrong. I'm sorry, Beauty. I didn't mean to hurt you."

My chest goes tight and warm and fuzzy all at once. I lean

down to wrap my arms around his shoulders, pressing my face into his hair to let him know that he's forgiven.

Then I tug him to his feet and wrap my arms properly around his waist, breathing in the sweat and faded cologne—the smell of Vibes, I know now.

"I just want to know why," I tell him as I press my face into his shoulder, swaying gently with him despite the pounding beat.

Prince goes still, and I pull away enough that I can see his face. And the look I see there… it makes me stop on the spot, too.

I just want to hug him until all the pain goes away.

"I… I'm used to getting rejected. With a face like this, you know…?"

My jaw slowly drops.

Fuck. Really? I never would have guessed that he felt insecure that way.

No wonder it hurt so much when I didn't stand up for him in the bar—or just now, at home.

I happen to think his face is suited perfectly to his soul. Maybe it's not conventionally beautiful, all artificial and smooth and perfect… but it's intense in exactly the right way. Every wrinkle and line is its own story.

As far as I'm concerned, he's fucking gorgeous.

"You—what? No. What?" Prince gives me a sheepish smile, but I'm not going to let him cut me off yet. "No," I tell him again, poking a finger into his chest. "I don't know what made you hold yourself back, but you're not allowed to use that excuse again."

He blinks at me like he's startled, and then he slowly frowns. "Yeah. Maybe you're right. It was something else…" he muses, rubbing a hand over his chin.

I think I know what it is, too.

Prince is easily among the hottest men in this room… so long as his face is this open and vulnerable. But I've just spent hours watching him look like a man hiding in the spotlight, keeping everyone happy but miles and miles away from him.

Maybe he's only been letting people see his walls, the dryness and sarcasm and distance. I saw flashes of it the first time we met at the bar. But I saw a lot more than that, too. And my heart aches for all the pain I didn't know about while we were in the dark.

"Listen," I tell Prince firmly, and he glances at me like he's surprised to hear so much resolve in my voice. "I want you. I don't want to hide you away in the dark. I want everyone to know that I want you—even my friends, when they're being overprotective jerks."

Prince manages a shaky smile at that.

It's my turn to try to sink to my knees.

Prince loops an arm around my waist, holding me up like it's second nature.

This is the man who took my innocence and my heart and gave me my future. No matter how much I squirm to tell him that I'm not falling and it's a deliberate maneuver… he can't even think of letting me go, just in case.

I clutch his shirt tightly in both hands instead, staring into those beautiful stormy eyes.

"I'm sorry, Prince. I swear I won't do that to you ever again." My throat is tight, and tears are leaking down my nose again. "I'm done trying to sleepwalk through life. I promise. If you want me…" I draw a deep, shaky breath. "I want you. God, do I ever want you."

Prince leans in, and even though I pucker up, he's not

aiming for my lips. He kisses my nose, my forehead, both cheeks, my eyes… all over my face, until my tears slow down.

He thinks I can't see the tears in his eyes that way… but I can. When he finally leans down into me, resting his forehead on my shoulder, I grab my chance to hold him tight.

"Oh, Beauty. I've been waiting a lifetime to hear someone say that."

"I know," I whisper as his hands come to rest gently on my back, and mine on his. We're swaying gently again, ignoring the beat thrumming through our chests, and the crowd, and everything besides each other.

At last, I mumble, "It's Briar."

"Briar." Prince smiles slowly. "My beautiful Briar. I'm Prince. But I guess you know that now…"

I can't help cracking a grin. "Yeah. I think I saw your face somewhere. A wanted poster, maybe?"

"Funny," Prince snorts dryly.

I giggle, and at last I can't hold back the ear-to-ear grin. "Prince," I repeat, just like he did. "*My* Prince."

"Always," Prince swears, and then he pulls away from me to take both of my hands. "I'm free to go home." Then a mischievous sparkle appears in his eye. "Or the darkroom is right that way… or we can do it against this wall, if you're not too shy…"

"Shut *up*," I snort with laughter. "I thought—"

"Oh, I know what you thought, Beauty." Prince chuckles. "You have *far* too many dirty thoughts for a face as pretty as yours."

He's still grinning wickedly as I drop one of his hands and spin around to march for the entrance of this room. I don't remember where I'm going, but I know where I want to go: home.

"Too much time in the dark for you lately?" Prince asks, taking over leading the way before I can even ask.

"Yeah," I admit, glancing up at him. "I want to meet you in the light." Then I blush. "You can surprise me in the dark for round two, later. At home."

"Perfect."

Prince pulls me against him right in the middle of the doorway and kisses me so deeply that he almost bends me in two. I'm dimly aware of the whoops and hollers and cheers from nearby—and I can't stop blushing as I let go of everything.

At last, I sink into Prince's arms, and he catches me. He sweeps me clean off my feet, and even if I squeak with surprise, I trust him to know what I need. In yielding to him, I'm showing Prince—telling everyone, too, even without saying a word—what I need and want.

I want him. I need him to be the beast, the prince, *and* the fairy for me.

And I'm going to be his Beauty. I'm going to tell him every day that I want him. And I'm going to mend his heart until he forgets how to be wicked at all… except in the middle of the night, when I need it the most.

"Your castle or mine?" I ask him playfully.

He grins down at me. "You've shown me yours. I'd like you to see mine. It's on the second floor, so there's no climbing into windows. And definitely no climbing out of windows."

"We don't need windows anymore," I whisper. "Take me there, Prince."

I wrap my arms around Prince's shoulders, and he carries me outside into the warm, rainy night.

CHAPTER

Fifteen

BRIAR

"Tell me what feels good."

Prince is crouching between my legs as I sit on the edge of his bed. He tugs my second boot off and sets it aside, then rests his palms on my shins.

"Fuck," I moan.

Everywhere Prince touches, sparks fly. Even places I didn't know could be erogenous are quickly turning out to be hotspots under his skilled hands.

"Or you can show me," Prince teases, glancing pointedly between my legs. "That works, too."

I know, I know. My toga is barely functional anymore. The stupid costume has ridden up to the tops of my thighs. Without any underwear… there's just no way to hide what's poking up under the thin fabric.

I bet he can see my hard-on from underneath.

That thought actually makes the blood rush down south even faster as heat scorches my cheeks.

I fumble with the stupid pin at the shoulder, and then I just grab the damn thing by the hem. "Let me get this—"

"Whoa," Prince grabs my wrists as fast as that, pulling my hands away from the toga as he gives me a stern glance. "You haven't given me a lot of ways to undress you tonight. I've got to make every piece of clothing count."

Then, he lets go of my wrists and gives me one solid shove to the chest. I flop back onto his bed with a squeak, my hands flying over my head, but Prince stays right where he is, kneeling on the floor at the edge of the bed.

"Oh my God," I breathe out as his hands slide up the insides of my thighs. I'm squirming underneath his palms, fighting for every breath. "Fuck, fuck, fuck…!"

I'm pretty sure I know why he's there now. I can't stop imagining what it's going to be like to have his hot mouth around my needy cock. I don't think I'll have any problems getting there tonight—in fact, I'm not even sure I'm going to have a refractory period between rounds.

"For example, I take it you like this." Prince's touch slows as he rubs down across the backs of my legs and up again. My toga is riding further and further up—and there's already a wet spot of precum showing against the white fabric.

Fuck. I'm so turned on it hurts.

"*Please,*" I pant for breath.

"Is that a yes?" Prince stops with his hands on my inner thighs, just short of where I so desperately want his fingers to go. My cock twitches in midair, but he doesn't budge, waiting for my answer.

"Yes, yes, *yes!*"

Prince hums with satisfaction. "Good. You like being touched slowly… treasured and teased."

I drag my hands down my face to cover it, blushing furiously into my palms. Is he going to make me listen to a description of all my turn-ons? I'm pretty sure he is. And given how much I'm burning up... I think I'm going to like it.

"What else do you like?" Prince murmurs. He slowly hooks his thumbs into the hem of the toga, dragging it up across my cock until I'm panting open-mouthed at the soft, teasing sensation.

"Off," I moan.

Prince laughs, but he tugs it all the way up to my waist in one quick move, and over my head in another.

And I'm naked, splayed across his bed as he sinks back into a crouch between my legs. He gazes past my hard cock and up the length of my body, sizing me up like a prince with his kingdom.

I'm his.

"What else do you want, Beauty?"

I lick my lips nervously, trying to cast my mind back to the last couple of encounters. He already knows how to make me lose my mind with pleasure.

"I... I don't know yet," I murmur. "I haven't found out."

I peek through my fingers to find Prince gazing up at me thoughtfully. One hand rests on my thigh, the other on my hip, his fingers framing the base of my cock—which twitches hard as soon as I notice that.

Fuck.

I want to tell him, even if I'm shy about it. I want him to know everything.

"That night was my first time," I whisper, my hands sliding down to my chest.

"Oh," Prince breathes out, his eyes widening as he stares at me. "Seriously? First time *ever*? And you... I... *we...*" he trails off, mouth still hanging open.

It's hilarious, the look on his face. He's definitely remembering everything he did to me in the moonlight—more forceful and unrelenting than I'd ever dared to fantasize about. But if he's having second thoughts, then I'm glad he didn't know back then, because I wouldn't change a single thing.

"It wasn't bad, for a first time," I tell him, stifling my giggle. "So I know I like that. Everything else, we'll just have to see."

"Jesus, Beauty," Prince whispers, shaking his head as he recovers his wits. "Good thing you're such a fast learner. We've got a lot of ground to cover."

Then he presses a kiss on the inside of my thigh, and I melt into a puddle right there under his hands. Heat throbs through me, and with every kiss—further and further up my thigh—I moan louder.

It doesn't feel as strange as I thought it would, showing all my reactions. I've spent so long practicing lying still in the moonlight. I never imagined that my fantasy prince would want to see my reactions—study me so closely in the light, so he can please me in a thousand different ways.

"I want to wake you up in every single way," Prince breathes out, and my cheeks turn scarlet with delighted heat.

"Yes, please," I breathe out. "Every way you can think of."

I love to watch him at work, kissing and touching and stroking me, glancing up to see how much pleasure I get, and from what. In the light, it's all right there—the biting wit he uses to hide how much he cares, his devotion and loyalty, and the ghosts of all his old fears about not being enough.

Even Prince's touch holds a little more magic, now that I can see all the care he puts into everything he does.

I want to give him everything.

If that means setting myself free to moan and giggle and

gasp as his hands wander across my body, stroking and holding and rolling body parts this way and that, kissing them and licking them and nibbling them… I'm more than happy to be the vessel for all of his wicked dreams.

Fuck. I'm floating in outer space, my head spinning from every little brush of his skin against mine.

"Mmhmm?" Prince murmurs, his lips against my hip. "This spot?"

"All of it," I admit in a giggle. "It all just feels good now. Because it's you."

I can hear Prince's smile in his reply. "I feel the same, Beauty. Exactly the same."

Then—without even a moment of warning—Prince's fingers close around my shaft, tightening gently just enough that I squeak and squirm underneath him.

"Fuck!"

"Mm*hmm*," Prince murmurs, chuckling like he was expecting that. Slowly, ever so slowly, he drags his fist to the base of my shaft and then back up again, twisting his stroke a little as he goes.

Oh, and it's a thousand times better than my own hand ever was. I don't know what magic is in his touch, but I want more of it. So, so much more.

"Fuuuuck…!"

"Mmhmm. Waiting makes it better, doesn't it?" Prince purrs smugly.

"Y-Yes… ohmyfucking—" I trail off into another squeak as Prince rubs his thumb across the tip. "Fuck!"

Prince grins. "Even if we see each other every night, you're going to have to follow my rules. Some nights, I'll tell you what you're allowed to do. Other nights, you're not going to cum. But I will, if and as I choose. All right?"

Fuck fuck *fuck*, I want him to keep talking dirty like this.

"Yes, Daddy," I choke out my words, throbbing hard against his palms. "Whatever you say."

"Good boy," Prince murmurs. "Whenever I let you cum, it'll be so good you remember it for days. It's so much more sensitive now, isn't it? You're happy to obey me, aren't you?"

I groan sharply, my heart thudding against my ribs as he strokes his hand slowly up and down my shaft. "Fuuuck…!" My toes curl into the bed, but however hard I pant for breath, he isn't speeding up the way I would.

The unhurried pace is so much better than all of my desperation put together.

"Hm?" Prince prompts me, reminding me that he's waiting for an answer.

I choke out another little whimper. "Thank you for—for making me obey," I breathe out. "For knowing what I needed before I did… so I could figure it out on my own…"

Prince smiles up at me. "And what did you figure out, Beauty?"

I lick my lips, peeking through my lashes again. "That I need you. That I *want* you. And… and I like you. A lot more than I realized."

The air rushes out of Prince's lungs, right across the tip of my cock. I can't help a shudder, a loud moan, at the maddeningly, yet deliciously teasing sensation.

"And—that," I choke out. "I—I want that."

Prince grins. "Then you can have it, my love."

Did I just hear—

Oh, fuck!

Prince's mouth slides around the tip of my cock, tight and hot and wet in a way I could only ever imagine. He envelops me without hesitation, and all I can do is cry out shamelessly as I grab his shoulders for dear life.

Even his deep chuckle vibrates through my shaft as Prince takes control of me in yet another way, bobbing his head slowly down to take me in an inch at a time. I'm already clinging to the very edge.

It's just about impossible to hold out now.

"I-I can't last long if you… oh!" I whimper. "Fuck! But my refractory period… won't be… very long…"

Prince lets my shaft pop out of his mouth and into the cool air, and I shiver with delight at the strange temperature shift. He curls his fingers around my hard-on, stroking slowly as he breathes his words across the flushed, sensitive skin.

"Long words like that don't belong in fairytales. I'm not doing my job right if you can use them."

"I didn't—ohhhhhhfuck!"

Prince takes my cock into his mouth and slams his head to the base of my cock, swallowing me in one hard, fast movement as he sucks his cheeks in. I can't even tell if I'm cumming, or if it just feels so good that I'm pulsating uncontrollably.

But he's doing it again and again, and everything besides Prince seems to slip away into a hazy blackness—

"Oh fuck, oh fuck, *now* I'm… I'm… Prince!" I cry out, throwing my head back into the pillow as my whole body clenches tight and releases at once.

I'm thrashing under him, my hips helplessly bucking as I spill my hot, sticky load all over his tongue. He just keeps on sucking me into his mouth, gulping every now and then, and every single time I hear it, I twitch all over again.

"Fuuuck," I breathe out as I collapse into the bed. "Fuck, *fuck…!*"

As I start to soften, Prince pulls away at last and scoots up the bed. I half-expect his fingers to slide into me, but… he's not doing that yet.

He just takes me in his arms and holds me, rubbing my back in soft, sweet circles as he kisses my hair.

"Oh, fuck," I breathe out as I roll into him, closing my eyes and breathing in the scent of him. "Oh my *fuck.*"

"You liked that, then," Prince murmurs with another deep chuckle that vibrates through my cheek.

I smile dizzily against him. "Mmhmm," I breathe out. "I really, really did. Oh my God. How did I get so lucky?"

"I was just thinking the same thing," Prince murmurs. As he shifts against me, I can feel his hard-on, too. It's still trapped in his pants, but it's definitely nestled against my thigh… and someone's going to need to do something about that.

I blink dizzily as I pull away from Prince to look him up and down. "Is it my turn to see you naked?"

Prince laughs abruptly, like I've startled him. Then his eyes soften into something warm and tender. "Would you like to?"

"This is my first chance to look at you in the light," I murmur, shyly smiling at him. "I'd fucking *love* to see you. And smell you. And taste you…"

Prince's eyes are dark and hungry. "And would you like to feel me inside you, too, my Beauty?"

My cheeks hot, I pull away from him to roll onto my back and bat my lashes, spreading my legs to invite him closer. "Whenever you please, Prince Charming," I whisper. "The door is always open. And if not, you can sneak through the window."

I'm finally learning what I want. And as long as I don't have to say it out loud *every* time, I'll be the happiest boy alive.

"That's lucky for both of us," Prince says with a slow grin, rolling over to straddle me. "Because there's nowhere I'd rather be."

And that makes two of us.

CHAPTER

Sixteen

PRINCE

I'VE NEVER FELT THIS TENDER—LIKE I'M ABOUT TO LAUGH, CRY, or maybe both at once.

But I can't hold back what I feel. With each breath we share, each kiss I press against my Beauty's lips, another crack in my heart mends. I'm deep inside my boy—and this time, I get to spend every second looking deep into his eyes.

And what I find there...

It doesn't just make my cock hard, although I *am* harder than I've ever been as I surge into him. No, the look on his face makes the walls around my heart soften and crumble away. At last, I'm giving in to the moment. I'm giving him everything I have.

And he wants it all.

Beauty has long since gotten hard again. I've got his wrists above his head to make him hold out so it feels better for him... and so we can make this last a little longer. But he's whimpering and squirming under me. He's clenching tightly around me with every stroke, and I can't deny him much longer.

As for me… I'm only hanging on by a thread.

Just having his eyes on mine as my Beauty embraces everything I give him, knowing that my desire is lighting him up… every moan I give is a confession that Beauty welcomes. He gathers them up like precious gems, and I get to watch this beautiful piece of his soul light up like never before.

I can't believe he gave me another chance. He saw the truth, and he forgave me—and forgiving him was the easiest thing I've ever done.

We've both learned our lesson. And that really is a fairy-tale come true.

I'm falling for him… or I already have. I don't know, but it doesn't matter, because every chapter of my fairytale yet to come is about my boy, my Briar, my one and only Beauty.

"Fuck," Beauty groans, rolling his head back as I drag the tip of my tongue along his throat. One kiss at a time, I work my way to his lips, and then I kiss him until he can hardly breathe.

I can tell how close he is. It's written all over his face. And I don't think I'm even going to need to touch him.

"P-Prince," Beauty whispers, his eyes flying open as he finally realizes the same thing. "I—I'm—ohhhh, fuck!"

"Yes," I growl against his lips, nipping the lower lip and swiping my tongue along it like the possessive prince he's always dreamed of. "Give me your pleasure. Cum for me, Beauty. Show me how much you love to be mine."

"Yours," Beauty echoes in a whimper. "And—and mine. My Prince."

I finally let go of his wrists, and he wraps his arms around my back, clinging on as tight as he can.

"Your Prince," I promise, cupping his cheeks. "Always. I'll be here whenever you want." Then I grin, because I know exactly what will get him over the edge he's so desperately clinging onto. I lean down to kiss behind his ear, and then I breathe out, "And whenever *I* want."

Briar throws his head back and whimpers in a tone that makes me see stars. Or maybe that's the way he's clenching around my surging cock, his body tightening in uncontrollable little shivers as his climax slams into us both.

"Mmmmnh…!" Beauty cries out, and watching it on his face, I can't hold back either.

"Beauty," I gasp roughly. "I'm gonna—"

"Cum in me," Beauty whimpers. "Make me yours. Please please please make me—ohhh fuuuck…!"

Together, we tumble over the edge into the blackness, until I don't know where his pleasure ends and mine begins. Our bodies are entwined too tightly to possibly tell, and I don't think it matters, anyway.

His pleasure *is* mine… today, and every day from now on.

All I can think about is my Beauty. His taste on my lips, his body wrapped around mine, his scent, the feeling of his skin—everything is Beauty, and everything is more beautiful than I could have imagined.

"Fuck," I breathe out hoarsely as I finally collapse next to him. My head is spinning, and sweat is dripping down my forehead, but I can't stand to be apart from his body heat. I pull him in as tightly as I can, holding him until I come to my senses enough to clean him up.

All I've got nearby is tissues, but I don't want to stop touching him for long enough to get a cloth. Not yet, anyway. Not tonight.

"S'that good?" Beauty murmurs as I settle on my side next to him, pulling him into my chest once more.

"Hm?"

"This. It's good…?"

I think that's a question and not a statement. "For me?"

Beauty giggles. "No. For the other prince who fucked me into next week. Yes, you."

I can't help a laugh. I didn't think he even had words left in him, let alone this much sass, but my Beauty just keeps on surprising me. "Better than good. It's what I've been fighting for… waiting for… all this time."

"To know and be known."

Was that Beauty murmuring in my ear, or my own thoughts? No, it was him. He's peeking at me through his lashes with a contented little smile on his lips.

"Yeah," I whisper, my throat suddenly tight and my voice thick. "To know and be known."

"Come here," Beauty murmurs, and I blink at him.

"I am—" I cut myself off and yelp as Beauty wraps every one of his limbs around me and holds on tight. "Okay, I wasn't *that* close."

"I want you this close," Beauty murmurs, his face pressed tightly against my chest—and I swear my heart melts into a puddle, right there in my chest.

He's so shy about what he wants, but he's always wanted me. Even from the first moment we met.

It takes a little wriggling before I can get my hand over to the light switch and turn out the lights for us both. But it's worth the work, because having Beauty need me so much makes me… well, I have to clear my throat a few times to stop the wetness in the corners of my eyes.

Outside my bedroom window, dawn is breaking.

"I guess you've made an honest Prince out of me," I breathe out.

"Mmm?"

"It takes a real beauty to turn a wicked fairy into a handsome prince," I murmur, tugging the covers up around both of us.

"Mmm." Beauty shifts a little bit, sticking his nose into my collarbone. "You're going to have to stop that."

It still takes me aback, the way he's already learning to tell me what he wants. "Stop… what?"

"Repeating the stories they tell you." Beauty yawns. "Sure, you're a fairy. But you aren't a wicked one. You're just afraid to let people see all the magic you've got. All the love you give people. On the dance floor and in my bedroom… and everywhere, I bet."

God. I really don't get to hide behind a mask with this one. "Yeah," I breathe out at last. "I guess I am."

"I saw it tonight. You took off the mask with me, and then you were fucking radiant." Beauty yawns again, rubbing his cheek against my chest as I stroke my hand gently through his soft curls. "I'm not the only beauty in the room, Daddy."

I can't quite come up with an answer to that. I just roll my head to the side against the pillow to gaze out the window at the slow break of morning's light.

But I think he's right. I have a lot that I've never given… a lot that I thought the world didn't want. But I don't have to hide any of my desires—Briar can stretch to fit them all.

And that's not just a euphemism.

When he looks at me, I think he sees someone I haven't yet met… the Prince I was always supposed to be. And just like I'm going to be the Daddy he needs to grow into the man he's meant to be…

I think he's holding on tight to that version of me, until I can see him in the mirror for myself.

And isn't that a little bit magic right there?

"Thank you," I whisper at last, but Beauty's breaths are finally slow, deep, and even. I think he's already drifting to sleep, and it won't be long before I follow suit.

Beauty isn't just the happily-ever-after I always wanted—he's my new beginning.

Epilogue

BRIAR, SIX MONTHS LATER

God, my right wrist is just killing me.

But as I stumble out from a long day of writing exams, I already know who's going to be waiting there for me.

My Prince—and he's holding two cups of coffee.

"A fruity little blueberry number for you, my love," he greets me, holding one out and leaning down for a kiss.

I lean backward and eye him. "Decaf?"

His eyebrows climb up, and he stares at me. "Of course. I know your sleep routine. I *made* your sleep routine, boy."

"Okay, okay," I giggle, tilting my face up to let him kiss me as I accept the cup of coffee. "Sorry, Daddy."

He grabs me by the ass until I squeak, pats me firmly, and lets go. "That's better," he murmurs, and we set off walking together. "So, how'd you do?"

"Pretty well, I think." I grin up at him. "Really well, actually."

Prince beams at me. "I know you did. You've been good as gold lately."

I bat my lashes up at him. "Yes, Santa Daddy. I don't want a stocking full of coal again this year."

"I'm not *that* old," Prince scowls at me, but he manages to crack a smile. He's starting to real about his age these days, and where he is in life.

Especially with how far he's come in the last six months. And I'd like to take a little credit for that, thank you very much. Ever since I told him to let down his walls… well, his career has taken off.

Plus, now that we're living together, he gets all the outlets he needs for that wicked streak I love so much.

"I know," I groan at him. "But I'm sure the fairies talk to the elves, who talk to Santa. You can pass on a message."

Prince snorts dryly. "Good save. So is it another meeting tonight? Who's this one with?"

"Uh…" It's getting hard to keep them all straight. almost reach for my phone before I remember. "Oh, right! The grad student who went into research."

"I thought you wanted to practice?"

"I did. I do. But research matters, too. There are so many kinks we just haven't studied at all," I tell him earnestly. "If I can help normalize it, I could make such a difference. And now that I can stay awake through stats class…"

"God, Beauty." Prince smiles crookedly, slipping his hand into mine. "You really *will* need your sleep if you're trying to change the scene from the top down *and* the bottom up."

I blush as I laugh. "I *will* choose one career path, I swear."

It's just exciting to care so much about what I do now—to find out all the ways I could do good, and make a real difference.

As we come to a halt in front of the campus cafe, Prince

squeezes my hand. "You don't have to choose forever. You have a lot of chapters ahead of you."

I beam up at him and stretch onto tiptoes so he can kiss me again. "I know. So, listen… I probably won't make it home before you're off to Vibes."

Prince smiles at me. "Or you can head home to bed, and I can pretend to sneak in like old times. I'll have to take the door, though. After how the Christmas lights went, I'm not climbing up that ladder again."

My giggle turns into a stifled snort when he glares at me. "Sorry. I'll hold the ladder next time. But in my defense, your ass *did* look really good…"

"Anyway," Prince says, sparing us another round of this ongoing debate over ladder safety, "it's okay if you can't come tonight."

"No, no," I shake my head, and then I shove my coffee into his hand. "I might not last the whole night, but I came prepared."

"You… what?"

I'm ridiculously proud that he's headlining the Vibes Christmas party, and I'm not going to miss it for the world. Even after my all-important final exams. Prince's eyebrows climb up as I unbutton the first few buttons of my shirt.

Then he sees what's underneath: a bright red harness.

"I sat through back-to-back exams in this. I'm going to put it to good use. But I didn't expect the jock strap to be so distracting," I sigh as I button my shirt back up.

Prince stares, opens his mouth as if to say something, and finally rubs his forehead. "Red? Are you sure?"

I tilt my head and take my coffee back to finish the last few sips. "For Christmas!"

Prince's lips twitch. "Ah. Not fisting."

"What?!"

Shit. It's the color thing again, isn't it? I forgot about that...

Prince's eyes sparkle as he leans down to kiss me. "You've come a long way this year, but there's always more left to learn. I hope you find some answers tonight, Beauty."

"Oh, I already have," I smile up at him until he can't help but smile back. "But I'll find even more answers today. Or one of my other... um, five meetings, I think?"

"Five?!"

"I spent three years avoiding the thought of my career path," I shrug ruefully. "I've got a lot of catching up to do."

Prince relents and smiles at me. "Well, I'm proud of you for waking up and smelling the coffee... even if you're running at ninety miles an hour. It's probably good for me, trying to keep up with you."

"You're welcome," I wink at him, and he smacks my ass again as I giggle.

In all the chaos of the last few months, Prince has picked up every piece I couldn't keep together on my own. Whenever I need him, he's there. Usually before I even know I need him.

Prince keeps my life together, my faith strong, my heart full... and my ass un-fisted.

Thank God for that.

"Thanks, Daddy. And good luck tonight," I tell him, beaming up at him. "I'll see you later."

He just winks at me. "And you'll feel me even later, Beauty."

Ohhhhmygod.

It's all I can do not to drop my coffee cup right in the snow as Prince leans down for a kiss, winks at me, and then strides off down the sidewalk.

At last, I turn to the coffee shop to face another meeting, and the future that no longer feels like it's written for me. Nowadays, I get to decide what I want. And when I don't, it's because I decided that, too.

I'm wide awake for the beautiful fairytale of my life, and I don't want to miss a single minute of it.

About the Author

E. Davies writes feel-good, low-angst romance that never fades to black when the going gets good! Born in Canada, after 16 moves and counting, Ed has finally put down roots in north London.

He emerges from his writing nest to coo over fuzzy animals, flee from cute guys, dance through the streets with his chosen family, put together fierce looks, and—most of all—befriend local flowers.

FOLLOW E. DAVIES ONLINE:

amazon.com/author/edavies
bookbub.com/authors/e-davies
facebook.com/edaviesauthor
goodreads.com/edavies
instagram.com/edaviesauthor

Also by E. Davies

SUNRISE ISLAND BROTHERS

Collide, Stranded, Adrift, Unmoored

TWISTED

Golden Boy, Beauty Sleep

HART'S BAY

Hard Hart, Changed Hart, Wild Hart, Stolen Hart

SIGNIFICANT BROTHERS

Splinter, Grasp, Slick, Trace, Clutch, Tremble

RILEY BROTHERS

Buzz, Clang, Swish, Crunch, Slam, Grind

BROOKLYN BOYS

Electric Sunshine, Live Wire, Boiling Point

F-WORD

Flaunt, Freak, Faux, Forever, Freedom

AFTER

Afterburn, Afterglow, Aftermath

SHARED UNIVERSES

Rosavia Royals: Barely Regal

Men of Hidden Creek: Shelter, Adore, Miracle, Redemption

Vino & Veritas: Limelight

AND MORE...

For a complete list of available titles by E. Davies:

edaviesbooks.com/books

www.ingramcontent.com/pod-product-compliance
Lightning Source LLC
Chambersburg PA
CBHW031252210726

48287CB00003B/998